H. G. Wells Secret Agent

ALEX SHVARTSMAN

UFO Publishing
Brooklyn, NY

PUBLISHED BY:

UFO Publishing
1685 E 15th St.
Brooklyn, NY 11229

Copyright © 2015 by Alex Shvartsman

Cover design: Jay O'Connell

ISBN: 978-1514638484

Visit us on the web

www.ufopub.com

ALSO AVAILABLE BY ALEX SHVARTSMAN

EXPLAINING CTHULHU TO GRANDMA AND
OTHER STORIES

AS ANTHOLOGY EDITOR

UNIDENTIFIED FUNNY OBJECTS

UNIDENTIFIED FUNNY OBJECTS 2

UNIDENTIFIED FUNNY OBJECTS 3

COFFEE: 14 CAFFEINATED TALES OF THE
FANTASTIC

DARK EXPANSE: SURVIVING THE COLLAPSE

.

CONTENTS

THE CASE OF THE WEATHER MACHINE

H. G. WELLS felt like he was on top of the world as he strolled through the Armorial Hall of the Winter Palace. A who's who of the St. Petersburg's elite mingled under the enormous chandeliers. Conversation, laughter, and music blended into a pleasant cacophony. Gentle sunlight bathed the hall through windows atop the balcony and reflected off the gilded columns. All of it created a storybook atmosphere the likes of which the young Englishman could only dream of until a few months ago.

Wells held his head high as he made his solitary way across the hall. He didn't look back, but out of the corner of his eye he noticed how the conversation ceased briefly as he passed by, and how these exemplars of Russian high society stole glances at him, sensing a whiff of mystery and danger. He imagined how all these dolled-up women desired him and the men pictured themselves in his place. He was enjoying himself beyond measure, and almost regretted it when a servant came to whisk him away to the most important meeting of his fledgling career.

He followed his guide out of the hall, the sounds of the party becoming gradually muted as they made their way through a patchwork of smaller rooms and staircases until they reached a massive cherry wood door. The servant nodded for Wells to go in and positioned himself to wait, a few steps down the corridor.

Wells touched a tiny marble inserted into his ear which allowed him to understand Russian and translated his own speech. The Ministry had appropriated a handful of such devices from a time traveler they had recently captured. Improbably, the woman from the future had called this gadget "the Babel fish," despite its apparent lack of any ichthyic qualities. Wells inhaled deeply and opened the door.

He entered a spacious study. One wall was lined with bookcases filled with weighty tomes. Directly ahead of him a window took up most of the wall, offering a magnificent view of the Neva River. And against the third wall sat a massive mahogany writing desk inlaid with intricate carvings: a desk fit for a monarch to run the affairs of Europe's largest empire.

The man sitting behind the desk, however, was not the tsar. He looked to be in his sixties, his gray hair cut short, contrasting with a thick, full mustache and beard. "So you're the one MacLean sent," said the man after studying his visitor for a few moments.

"Herbert George Wells, agent of the Ministry of Preternatural Affairs, at your service." Wells wasn't entirely certain if he should salute or bow, so he nodded to the older man and held himself at attention.

"And why is it you are here, Mr. Wells?"

"An audience," said Wells. "I was sent to meet with His Imperial Majesty—"

"No," the man behind the desk interrupted.

"Beg pardon?"

"No, you don't get to meet with the tsar." The older man leaned forward. "The political star of your boss, Ms. MacLean, must truly be at its zenith, risen high since I met her in London a few years ago. She dispatches emissaries to the courts of Europe and issues orders to those clearly above her station. But she has overreached, demanding a royal audience for a British spy. My name is Nikolai Bunge, Chairman of the Cabinet of Ministers. Your agency's clout buys you a few minutes of my very reluctant attention, and nothing more. So I say again, why are you here?"

"The Ministry represents more than the interests of the British Empire," said Wells. "Modern science has proven that there's far more to the world than was previously dreamt of in our philosophy. There are terrible threats just around the corner, nesting among the stars, in other realities, and in the vastness of time. Threats we're ill-prepared to face. Queen Victoria created the Ministry to arm the human race against the future. The twentieth century is when everything changes. And we've got to be ready."

Bunge frowned and made a show of opening and checking his gold pocket watch. "I gave you five minutes and you already squandered some of it on a speech that served no purpose other than to make yourself feel important. Kindly get to the point, I have matters of state to attend to."

"The weather machine," Wells blurted out. "We know that Russia has a secret weapon capable of altering weather patterns. This technology is of considerable interest to the Ministry, and I've been authorized to negotiate for the opportunity to examine it."

Bunge laughed. "A weather machine? We have no need of such things. Our cold winters are weapon enough. Just ask Napoleon, or any other invader who had suffered the misfortune of their armies being caught on Russian soil after the snow begins to fall."

"Are you certain? Ms. MacLean had it on very good authority—"

Bunge waved him off. "I have no interest in that upstart's delusions. Who does she think she is, sending a man-child, barely old enough to shave, and expecting the attention of the monarch himself? No, you've wasted enough of my time with your tales of fantastical machines and otherworldly foes. Go back to your master and tell her to keep her odd affairs out of Russia."

BACK IN THE ARMORIAL HALL, Wells sought to soothe his bruised ego with strong spirits. He approached one of several bars set up for the guests. He waited for the bartender to finish serving a glass of sparkling wine to an attractive blonde.

"Have you got any gin?" Wells asked.

The bartender shook his head. "Vodka," he said curtly. "Seven different flavors."

"Obviously," said Wells. "Very well. I'll have a vodka mixed with a shot of the Kina Lillet you've got over there." Out of the corner of his eye he noticed the blonde watching him with interest. Perhaps this day wasn't entirely ruined yet. "This mixture is my own invention; I'm going to patent it when I think of a good name. Make sure it's stirred, not shaken. Wouldn't want the drink to be weak."

He turned toward the blonde and flashed his best smile. "My name is Wells. Herbert Wells."

The blonde giggled and walked off, carrying her glass. Wells sighed as he watched her go. Things really weren't working out in the way he had imagined. He waited for his drink, composing excuses for Ministra MacLean in his head. His first mission for the Ministry was shaping up to be his last.

Wells took a swig of the proffered cocktail and coughed violently. The drink turned out to be far more potent than he had anticipated.

"You should have added lemon to that. I take a slice whenever I have to drink Cognac. Makes the vile stuff taste almost tolerable."

Wells looked up at the tall, immaculately groomed young man advising him, and swallowed the biting remark he was about to make. Standing in front of him was the heir to the Russian throne.

"Prince Nicholas!" Wells put his drink on the counter. "It's an honor to meet you, sir. I'm—"

"Herbert Wells. Yes, I overheard." The Russian royal smiled into his beard. "Just as I overheard your conversation with Bunge. I must apologize for him; the man is a brilliant economist and a competent bureaucrat, but he is certainly no diplomat."

The prince must have seen the confusion on Wells's face, so he clarified: "Bunge's office has very thin walls. One learns such things growing up in this place. Come, we have much to discuss."

For the second time in the span of an hour, Wells was led

to the private rooms of the Winter Palace.

The Russian *tsarevich* was eighteen, only a couple of years younger than Wells. Surely someone like him would be more receptive to the modern realities in which the Ministry dealt than a stuffy old minister who reminded Wells of his school's headmaster back in England.

"I've been following the news of Ministry exploits with a great deal of interest," said Prince Nicholas. "Special agents armed with a plethora of futuristic gadgets – it's all very exciting. Tell me, Wells, is the life of an adventurer everything you hoped it'd be?"

Wells was among a small number of students recruited straight out of the Royal College of Science by Sue Ann MacLean. The Ministry's chief had somehow acquired a copy of "The Chronic Argonauts," a short story about traveling through time, which Wells was shopping around to newspaper publishers. MacLean said she was impressed with Wells's imagination and didn't want the young man to waste his talents on creating fictions. The trip to St. Petersburg was the first time he has ever traveled outside of the British Isles. But it wouldn't do to let the *tsarevich* know that.

"It is an honor and a privilege to guard the world against outside threats," said Wells.

"The world or England? For all the talk of protecting everyone, it is Queen Victoria's empire that holds in its vaults the wondrous gadgets you agents fetch from across the globe."

"When the time comes, arbitrary borders won't matter," said Wells. "Our true nationality is mankind."

"Very well," said Prince Nicholas. "England doesn't hold the monopoly on scientific wonders. I will allow you to examine Russia's secret weapon, the weather machine. But only if you and the Ministry help me with a small matter first."

"What is it that you need us to do?" asked Wells.

Prince Nicholas Romanov of Russia looked Wells straight in the eye. "Find the men who are trying to kill me."

BACK AT THE BRITISH EMBASSY, Wells used one of the Ministry's infamous devices to reach out to his friend and mentor.

He cranked the dials of the unwieldy contraption filling the most private room of the embassy building. Delicate gears rotated and clicked as it came to life. The large apparatus worked on the same principle as the newly invented telephone, but was capable of transmitting one's voice across the ether without the use of wires. MacLean bragged that Ministry scientists were on the verge of making a compact travel version of this device, one that could fit into a large carriage. Even at present size, it was among the most useful tools in the Ministry arsenal. Queen Victoria had ordered each of her key embassies outfitted with one.

The contraption emitted a high-pitched noise as it established a connection to London's fledgling telephone network. "Please connect me to Mr. Doyle," Wells told the operator.

Wells was glad to hear the voice of a friend, even if it was distorted by static. He explained about his meeting with Prince Romanov.

"The *tsarevich* wants me to find the leaders of a radical socialist group called the People's Will," said Wells. "They have waged war against the Romanovs for years. In '81 they had quite a coup, managing to assassinate Nicholas's grandfather, Tsar Alexander II."

"Radical indeed," said Doyle. "Wasn't Alexander the most liberal monarch Russia has ever had? Their version of Abraham Lincoln, who finally emancipated the serfs? His successor isn't nearly so progressive."

"Be that as it may, they seem to have developed a taste for hunting royals. The People's Will made a number of attempts on the current tsar's life, explosives their weapon of choice. The Romanovs have been forced to move to a more secure home, with Winter Palace deemed too large and approachable, difficult to protect on a daily basis. Currently it's only used for official functions. And now, it seems, the People's Will have set their sights on Prince Nicholas. The prince has been forced into hiding until this threat is dealt with."

Doyle was silent for a moment and Wells pictured the senior agent taking a puff of his pipe as he mulled over the information. "I see. We don't generally prefer to meddle in the affairs of states, but foiling an assassination plot against the prince would gain the Ministry a most valuable ally."

"The Russian secret police couldn't find these people," said Wells. "What hope do I have, with no useful contacts or local knowledge in St. Petersburg?"

"Elementary, my dear Wells," said Arthur Conan Doyle. "The prince sought out your help because of the stellar reputation and notoriety enjoyed by our organization around the globe. It stands to reason that, should you publicly express certain political views, the likes of the People's Will shall also reach out to you of their own volition."

Doyle, now in his late twenties, was a Ministry field agent

from the very beginning, when Queen Victoria established the organization in '82. Wells and he had become fast friends, and the veteran agent's advice was always sound.

"For all the fancy toys in your arsenal, the Ministry's reputation is your finest weapon," Doyle reiterated in his slight Scottish accent. "Use it well, my friend."

"DEMOCRACY IS THE ROAD TO SOCIALISM," announced Wells, his voice slurred by the several drinks he had to imbibe in order to stay in character.

This was the second bar he had visited that evening, a sort of dive where poor workers and students potentially sympathetic to the People's Will came to drink. Over the past several days Wells had made a tour of such establishments, quoting Marx and drawing attention to himself wherever he went. His progressive views were well received by the proletariat, but the people he met were well-meaning and earnest. They yearned for social change but weren't the sort who would associate themselves with terrorists. Doyle's plan wasn't working.

A man smelling of cheap beer tapped Wells on the shoulder. "You the Englishman revolutionary?"

Wells nodded, satisfied. Perhaps the persona he had been building was finally paying dividends.

"Got some like-minded friends who are keen to meet you," said the man. "Will you follow me?"

The man led Wells into an alley behind the bar, where two others were waiting.

"I hear you're the foreigner who's been talking about the redistribution of wealth," said one of the men.

"That's right. The cause of socialism is a global one," Wells replied.

"Then you won't mind giving us your wallet and your watch." The man smirked and drew a knife, moonlight reflecting off its wide blade.

Two of the mugger's friends moved to block the way back toward the bar, so Wells surprised them by rushing at the one holding the knife. He tackled the man, pushing him off to the side. The mugger swung his weapon as he fell, managing a long, shallow cut on Wells's left arm, just below the shoulder. Doing his best to ignore the sharp pain, Wells ran deeper into the dark alley, all three of his assailants in pursuit. Seconds later, his path was blocked. The alley terminated in a dead end.

Wells spun around, viscous liquid seeping through the cut in his shirt's sleeve, his back against cold bricks of the windowless wall. Unarmed and outnumbered three to one, he prepared to face his enemies.

The three muggers edged toward him cautiously, like a pack of jackals. Thankfully, only one of them had a knife. The trio was so intent on Wells, that they didn't notice another man approach them from behind.

The newcomer was young and very tall, sporting an unruly mop of dark hair, and stubble where most Russians would have a beard. He was too well-dressed to be in league with the other three. With the muggers concentrating on Wells, the tall man was able to walk up right behind the knife-wielding ruffian and bludgeon him with a piece of copper pipe he had pulled out from under his coat.

The mugger went down like a sack of beets, landing on the pavement with a loud *oomph*. Wells lunged at the nearest remaining opponent, while his unexpected ally engaged another. The four men exchanged blows under the moonlight, but with odds now evened, the bandits were no match for a trained Ministry agent and his rescuer. They fled, ignobly leaving their friend lying unconscious on the ground, his face in a puddle.

"Thank you." Wells extended his hand. "You fight well."

"Had no choice but to learn. I grew up with two older brothers." The man smiled and shook Wells's hand. "My name is Anton Chekhov. I'm a columnist for *New Times*."

"My name is Wells. Herbert—"

"Yes, I know who you are, Mr. Wells. I've been following your exploits in St. Petersburg with great interest. But we can talk about that after your wound is tended to. Come, my apartment is only a few blocks away."

WELLS WINCED as Chekhov expertly cleaned and bandaged the cut.

"It's only a flesh wound," Chekhov declared. "Keep the bandages clean and it will heal up nicely."

"You seem to know your way around a medicine bag," said Wells.

Chekhov's one-room apartment was filled with books and handwritten manuscripts. There was a hunting rifle hanging on the wall. A modified Remington typewriter with Cyrillic keys occupied the desk in the center.

"I should hope so," said Chekhov. "I'm a physician by trade."

"A doctor *and* a newspaper writer? You're a man of many talents."

"Medicine is my lawful wife and literature is my mistress; when I get tired of one, I spend the night with the other."

Chekhov grinned as he tightened the bandage. "Plays and short stories are my true passion, but writing for Russia's largest newspaper is what pays the bills."

"Is that why you happened to be lurking in that alley? You wanted to write a story about me?"

"Why would you be surprised? A British agent who is admitted at the Winter Palace, and yet so unsubtly seeks to connect with the revolutionary underground? That's a fascinating story, even if I don't have all the facts yet. I don't suppose you'd care to fill in the blanks?"

"Sorry," said Wells. "I'm grateful for your help, but I'm not at liberty to divulge the details of my mission. Part and parcel of being a secret agent, you understand."

"Of course," said Chekhov. "Every person lives his real, most interesting life under the cover of secrecy."

"Can I talk you out of writing about me altogether?"

"Sorry," said Chekhov. "Part and parcel of being a newspaper man."

"There may be a way for us to help each other," said Wells. "You said that writing fiction is your true passion. The Ministry has contacts in Russia, as we do elsewhere. We can place your plays and stories in front of all the right people. By this time next year you could be an award-winning author."

"You claim to wield quite an influence in literary circles."

"We must. Censoring classic works of fiction is often necessary in order to remove certain details we'd rather people didn't question. For example, the Ministry has worked diligently over the years to strike all mentions of the undead from books such as *Pride and Prejudice*."

"I do have a collection of short stories releasing soon..." Chekhov stroked his chin. "And all I'd have to do is avoid writing about your misadventures?"

"That. And there is one other thing," said Wells. "Help me get in touch with the People's Will."

IT TOOK CHEKHOV only a couple of days to make contact and set up a meeting.

The horse-drawn carriage took them past the factories and the working class neighborhoods of the city, past the sort of places where Wells might have expected to meet with the leaders of a terrorist group, and arrived on the campus of St. Petersburg University.

"Don't be surprised," Chekhov whispered as they entered the bowels of the Chemistry building. "Students are always on the front lines of whatever revolution is brewing."

They were led into a classroom where a group of young men sat around a pair of school desks that had been pushed together to create a makeshift table. It was littered with papers, beer and vodka bottles, and plates filled with an assortment of pickled herring, boiled eggs, and sliced rye bread. The smell of cigarette smoke permeated the air.

One of the men beckoned Chekhov and Wells over to the table and motioned for them to sit. He wiped his mouth with the back of his hand. "Welcome to the resistance. Would you like some potato chips?"

Wells studied the group of students gathered around the table. They reminded him of his classmates who spent many a late evening in groups such as this one, arguing about politics, philosophy, and women.

"We'd love to stay and chat, but we have an appointment to keep, with your leaders."

The students laughed.

"Relax, British," said the same man who spoke earlier. "You are meeting with them now." He was tall, gaunt, and possessed of a sort of manic energy usually induced by drinking too much coffee. He offered his hand to Wells. "Aleksandr Ulyanov, at your service."

Wells shook his hand. "You're the one in charge of the People's Will, then?"

"Why the surprise? It's all right for a Ministry agent to be very young, but not for a revolutionary leader?" Ulyanov leaned back, balancing his chair on its hind legs. "In politics, as in science, progress is the domain of the young. We embrace the modern ways of thinking, and devise stratagems that older generations are too rigid to appreciate."

You blow up innocent people with dynamite, you pompous prig. Wells kept his expression neutral and let Ulyanov pontificate.

"I understand why the Ministry reached out to us," said the terrorist. "Although your organization exists to prop up a rotting monarchy, your ranks are filled with bright young men and women, and you embrace the latest technologies in ways most of your countrymen do not. Your leaders understand that we're the future government of this country and, naturally, you want to ally yourself with the winning side." Ulyanov popped a potato chip into his mouth. "Question is, what is it that you can offer us?"

"This." Wells retrieved a vial filled with an oily, colorless substance from the inner pocket of his jacket. "The latest development from Alfred Nobel. This compound makes nitroglycerin seem safe and stable. What's more, you need only add a few drops to your dynamite in order to double the force of the explosion."

Wells handed the vial to Ulyanov who lifted it up to the

light, studying the liquid within.

"Have this tested." Ulyanov passed the explosive to one of his men. "There are technological marvels in our arsenal that far surpass mere bombs now," he told Wells. "Still, old methods are occasionally best."

"There's enough in that vial to supercharge a handful of bombs," said Wells. "If we reach an agreement, I can deliver a great deal more."

"You've chosen the right side, for now." Ulyanov's cold eyes stared through the British agent. "But the global revolution is coming. My kid brother, Vladimir, and all the other children will live to see the worker's paradise rise from the ashes of European empires, and that includes England. The Ministry will have to choose a side again, and I hope they make the right decision. We don't show mercy to our enemies." Ulyanov closed his fist slowly over the potato chip he was holding, crumbling it to dust.

CHEKHOV, WHO REMAINED QUIET during the meeting, was making up for it on the ride back from the university.

"This is not what I expected," said the playwright. "You're walking a dangerous path, trying to play both sides. And I certainly wouldn't have agreed to help you if I knew you were going to put powerful explosives in the hands of radicals."

"Don't panic," said Wells. "I'm not a villain. The compound I gave them will indeed strengthen the dynamite, but only temporarily. After a few hours, it will break down the glycerol molecules and turn any dynamite treated with it into duds."

"That's your plan?" asked Chekhov. "Once they figure it out, they can rid themselves of the spoiled dynamite and make more bombs."

"The chemical brew will work as advertised, long enough for them to conduct tests and become impressed," said Wells. "They will schedule another meeting, eager to receive a larger supply. Then all we have to do is to pass the information on to the prince. He can send the secret police to sweep them up."

"You seem awfully certain of your ruse."

"Dear Anton, a terrorist hasn't been born yet who could outsmart the strategic planners at the Ministry. All we have to do is to wait at the embassy, and maybe enjoy some supper. The People's Will shall take the bait soon."

Wells was right. A messenger delivered a note with the time and place of another rendezvous before they'd finished dessert.

WELLS AND CHEKHOV arrived at a luxurious villa on the outskirts of St. Petersburg. A well-manicured lawn surrounded a colonnaded two-story mansion. The prince was hiding out in style.

As soon as Nicholas had learned of their success, he'd summoned the pair to report to him directly. There was only a pair of military officers stationed inside the front entrance. A butler led them past the guards and through the mostly empty house. Nicholas opted for anonymity over heavy security to protect him against the People's Will.

"Well done," the *tsarevich* exclaimed upon hearing Wells's report. "I knew I could count on you to flush out and unmask my enemies. I shall order the arrest of this Ulyanov character immediately."

"I think not," someone said from behind Wells.

The British agent spun around, but found no one there.

"I warned you about what would happen were you to cross us, Wells."

The British agent recognized Ulyanov's voice, but couldn't figure out where it was coming from.

"Fortunately for us, your betrayal was well anticipated."

Wells's eyes widened as he watched a small vase float into the air from the mantle it was on, then fly across the room and shatter against the back wall.

"You thought yourself so clever, offering us a Trojan horse." A marble statuette followed the vase's trajectory and landed by the back wall with a dull thud. "But all we really needed you for was to lead us to whatever hidey hole the princeling used, so that we could kill him."

The next item to float was an elaborate gilded clock. And instead of the back wall, this one flew straight at Nicholas's head. The prince ducked and the projectile missed him by a hair. The clock landed behind him, splitting open and spilling fine gears onto the floor.

"What sorcery is this?" demanded Nicholas. "Are they employing some manner of poltergeist?"

"They're quite corporeal," said Chekhov. "The way the items are lifted, and the arcs they're thrown at, suggest there's human muscle behind it. We're being attacked by invisible men!"

"You're a clever Judas," said Ulyanov. "But there won't be a bag of silver in this for you. This is the only reward you deserve." There was a dull thud of an impact and Chekhov fell backward onto the floor. He sat up, dazed, a trickle of blood forming at the corner of his mouth.

"Take them!" ordered Ulyanov. Wells heard the sound of

multiple pairs of feet closing in.

Nicholas produced a Smith & Wesson Model 3 revolver and quickly unloaded the entire cylinder in the general direction of the incoming attackers. There was a scream and a thud. A pool of blood began to form on the floor, materializing in the air as it escaped from a still-invisible body.

Chekhov grabbed for a crystal vase and shattered it on the floor. "They're barefoot!" he shouted.

Wells nodded and edged closer to the broken glass, pulling the prince along. It seemed the assassins couldn't make weapons or any other items invisible, not even clothes or shoes. He was glad of any advantage, however small.

Nicholas, Chekhov, and Wells fought back-to-back, absorbing blows and swinging wildly. Ulyanov must not have counted on Nicholas's military training and Wells's Ministry skills, because the outnumbered trio was holding its own. There were shouting and footsteps outside as the *tsarevich's* security force arrived, drawn by the sound of gunfire.

Two officers burst in with rifles, but could find no targets. Then Chekhov dove for the fireplace and grabbed fistfuls of wood ashes. He threw the ashes up in the air and some of the residue settled on the invisible assailants, exposing their silhouettes. The officers did not need an invitation; they opened fire as soon as viable targets presented themselves. Wells and Nicholas followed the playwright's lead, throwing more ashes.

With tables turned against them, the remaining revolutionaries burst through the balcony doors and out of the building. Wells could swear he heard Ulyanov shouting curses as the terrorist leader scrambled away across the lawn, with armed men in pursuit.

The room, once again quiet, was littered with corpses, made visible by the layer of soot.

Nicholas kicked at the nearest body. "Rebel scum. The house of Romanov has ruled Russia for nearly three hundred years, and will surely continue to do so for three hundred more. It'll take far more than their parlor tricks to take down the future tsar."

Chekhov leaned against the wall, breathing heavily. "It seems Ulyanov wasn't merely bragging when he talked about having access to advanced science."

"Yes, I must make a report to the Ministry immediately," said Wells. "They'll want to know about this new threat. They'll want samples." He waved at the bodies.

"They can have the lot," said Nicholas. "I know my enemy now, even if I haven't seen his face. Every policeman in the Empire will be looking for Aleksandr Ulyanov. They'll question his known associates, friends, classmates – anyone he has ever exchanged a pair of sentences with. My operatives will root out the People's Will once and for all."

"It didn't go according to plan, but I'm glad to hear that you're satisfied," said Wells, breathing a sigh of relief. "I believe there's still the matter of the weather machine?"

"About that. You're welcome to examine the machine, just as I promised, but it's not here. I hope you enjoy long journeys; Siberia is beautiful this time of the year."

SUE ANN MACLEAN paced back and forth in her office, the typed copy of Wells's report clutched in her fist.

"This is a disgrace. A disaster. An utter embarrassment." MacLean squeezed the report, crumpling the pages. "I send you on a simple diplomatic errand, and what do you do? Poke at the beehive of Russian politics and very nearly get the heir to the throne killed in the process!"

"If I may, ma'am, I did accomplish the mission," said Wells. "I spent weeks traveling by Russian railroad, coach, and mule, all the way to the Central Siberian Plateau, near the border of Outer Mongolia. Prince Nicholas's letter granted me full access to the weather machine. I studied it thoroughly, and drew up blueprints, which I submitted to you as part of my report—"

"Damn the report," said MacLean. "I want to hear the answer from you. Tell me just how useful you think this technology is to the Ministry."

"It's not very useful to us," Wells admitted. "It's an impressive machine, a very large installation powered by steam and water current from the nearby river. But it was built in the 1700s and holds no new technologies that could be of immediate use to the Ministry."

Wells shifted his weight. MacLean hadn't invited him to sit down. "The machine is able to influence Western Russia's weather patterns because of its unique location. All they have to do is stall the invaders until winter, and then crank the gears up to eleven for extra cold and snow. Napoleon got to experience it personally in 1812. Russian winter truly *is* their secret weapon."

"And is there, in your opinion, a way for us to weaponize this technology?"

"Not that I can see, ma'am. Not unless the future battles are to be fought in the European territories of Russia."

"That's right. Your mission has failed to produce any useful results," said MacLean.

"I can hardly be blamed if the device *you* sent me to study wasn't all you expected it to be. And besides, what about the invisible men I had shipped to you from St. Petersburg?"

"By the time their bodies arrived, whatever chemical the People's Will scientists used had worn off. Our best people are still studying the cadavers, but they haven't found anything concrete so far."

MacLean quit pacing and poured herself a shot of brandy. "Under ordinary circumstances, this kind of a spectacular failure, on your first assignment no less, would be enough to end a career," she said. "You're very fortunate that we're short-handed." MacLean sipped from the glass and resumed pacing. "Nightingale recently retired, Stoker and Wilde are entirely consumed by a melodramatic rivalry over some woman, and Kipling is on a long-term mission in India."

MacLean sighed and finished the contents of her glass in one gulp. "So I can't afford to fire you, and therefore I shall do the next worst thing. I'm sending you to France.

"You're to oversee the giant space transceiver which Gustave Eiffel is building for us in Paris. This should keep you out of trouble for a few years."

"Yes, ma'am. As you wish, ma'am." Wells always wanted to visit Paris, but it wouldn't do to appear relieved in front of MacLean lest she change her mind and devise a less palatable punishment.

MacLean dismissed Wells with a wave. Wells headed for the door, but paused and turned around. "A question, ma'am, if I may?"

MacLean nodded.

"The weather machine. Are we going to let the Russians keep it? We may not be able to use it ourselves, but who knows, what if we end up on different sides in some future conflict and they use it against us?"

MacLean smiled at the question. "Now you're thinking like a true Ministry agent," she said. "But there is no reason to worry. I studied the blueprints you made and believe there is a fatal flaw in the design."

The Ministra of Preternatural Affairs refilled her glass and declared: "In my estimation, the Tunguska weather machine will blow itself up in the next twenty or so years."

THE CASE OF THE DIRIGIBLE HEIST

SPECIAL AGENT WELLS watched his French counterpart approach with a group of wealthy Parisians in tow. Pierre Curie ushered a trio of stone-faced men past the throngs of people enjoying a sunny afternoon and a chance to gawk at the pavilions and exhibitions in the final stages of being set up for the 1889 World's Fair. Curie chatted up his charges who seemed somewhat out of their element, lost in the frantic energy of people and events surrounding them, until finally the group joined Wells at the base of the colossal lattice tower recently constructed by Gustave Eiffel.

"Mr. Wells, meet the representatives of the Committee of Three Hundred," said Curie. "Monsieurs de Maupassant, Gounod, and Bouguereau."

The Committee of the Three Hundred, so named after the height of the Eiffel Tower, was the group of artists and influential socialites opposed to its construction. Wells faced the trio of the Committee's most outspoken members: Paris's most celebrated writer, composer, and painter.

"Thank you for agreeing to meet me here, gentlemen," said Wells.

De Maupassant stepped forward. "Monsieur Curie was very insistent," he said. Despite being the youngest of the three, he was clearly the group's leader. "In fact, I do not mind the excursion at all. This is presently my favorite spot in all of Paris."

"It is?" Gounod asked incredulously.

"The base of this structure remains the one place where I can still enjoy the view of my favorite city without seeing the giddy, ridiculous tower dominating its skyline like a gigantic black smokestack."

Wells recognized that, although they were a mere nuisance at this stage, these people stood a real chance of influencing the public opinion. Perhaps influencing it enough to pressure the French government into scrapping the tower after Eiffel's license ran out, in twenty years. This wouldn't do; Wells's superiors managed quite a coup, installing the world's most powerful communication device right in the heart of Paris, and they wouldn't have it jeopardized, not even two decades down the road. Wells was determined to set things right in time for the security summit.

"Your opprobrium for Mr. Eiffel's design is as well-known as it is eloquent." Wells waved at the enormous metal structure above them. "Truly, I admire how rapidly your committee has been gaining support at the highest levels of government. However, I cannot allow this propaganda campaign against the tower to continue. My superiors at the Ministry have tasked me with ensuring that nothing at all interferes with our plans."

"You dare summon us here and threaten us, in broad daylight?" William-Adolphe Bouguereau glared at the much younger Englishman from under his bushy gray eyebrows.

"Heavens, no," Wells told the painter. "Why antagonize someone when telling them the truth will accomplish the task?"

"The truth?" Charles-Francois Gounod, the composer, cocked his head.

"The nature of this structure," said Curie. "It isn't merely an architectural fancy."

"This enormous edifice was created to serve as what's called an antenna," said Wells. "A brand new technology developed by Dr. Heinrich Hertz in recent years, to transmit sound across great distances."

The five men looked up, to where the tip of the tower reached for the cloudless sky. A tiny dot of a dirigible was the only other object visible against the azure heavens.

Gounod was the first to break the spell. "I have it on good authority that the British spymasters have been using devices similar to what you're describing for years."

"This is true, even if we don't like to advertise it," said Wells. "But those are scavenged scraps, bits of science recovered from crashed spaceships and stalled time machines. Tools we are able to make use of without fully understanding their nature. But this," Wells pointed at the metal structure above him, "this is different. The epitome of modern thought, of human science—"

"Of bad taste," de Maupassant cut him off. "Newfangled technologies are all well and good, but why must you build this Aunt-Enna monstrosity in Paris?"

"Atop the Eiffel Tower is a very special transmitter

device," said Wells. "It allows us to monitor the skies and acts as an early warning system in case of an invasion from space."

"There are only a handful of focal points on our entire planet where such a device could be properly installed," added Curie. "Paris was, by far, the most logical choice."

"Giant antennae, alien invaders... This is all very incredible and difficult to believe," said Bouguereau.

"There are things out there that, until recently, were undreamt of in our philosophy." Wells spoke earnestly, maintaining eye contact with the Parisians. "Every government in the world is scrambling for ways to anticipate these new dangers and protect their citizens. This structure represents an unprecedented level of cooperation between numerous governments, coming together in recognition of the fact that guarding against outside threats is more important than their petty political squabbles. Surely this noble idea trumps matters of personal taste?"

The men stared upward again. The dirigible was hovering level with the topmost deck of the tower.

"The danger is real, if not very well known to the public," said Curie. "To me, tolerating one ugly structure is preferable to the idea of Martian tripods marching down the Champs-Élysées."

"Suppose it's true," said de Maupassant. "Suppose we accept this conspiracy theory of shadow treaties and space invaders. But then... why tell us?"

"We want to recruit you, of course." Wells smiled. "The Ministry has a history of working with writers and artists, men and women who possess the imagination and the open mind to accept the changing realities of our world." *Two birds with*

26

one stone, thought Wells. The creative types really did make the best agents, and recruiting these three would effectively put an end to the vocal resistance to the project he was supervising.

"I'm a loyal French citizen, young man," said Bouguereau. "I've no intention of joining Her Majesty's Secret Service."

"You'd be working for us," said Curie. "France has its own secret agency. The Deuxième Bureau may cooperate warmly with our friends from across the Channel, but rest assured that we're in charge on our own soil."

"I was far from convinced by your words," said Gounod. "But I'm rapidly becoming swayed by current events."

"How do you mean?" asked Wells.

"Whether or not you told us the truth, there's *something* up at the top that is worth stealing." Gounod pointed upward. "The Eiffel Tower is being robbed."

The dirigible had moored itself just under the tip of the tower with dozens of grappling hooks clutching at the metal beams. From the ground, Wells could make out tiny figures climbing across the ropes.

"They must be after the transmitter," shouted Wells. "Come on!"

He sprinted for the stairs. Curie followed, leaving the three Parisians behind.

Wells climbed the steep cast iron stairs of the tower as fast as he could, but he knew he would never make it to the top in time. With a structural height of over a thousand feet, the Eiffel Tower was the world's tallest man-made structure. Since the lifts were not yet operational, Wells estimated it would take him at least ten or twelve minutes to ascend that distance, even if he somehow managed to maintain his pace all the way up.

He heard the distant popping sounds of a firefight; the attackers must have engaged the security detail. Wells wondered if the guards would have the presence of mind to fire at the balloons keeping the dirigible afloat. A single well-placed shot might ignite the highly flammable hydrogen inside and bring the airship crashing down onto the Champs de Mars.

In less than a minute the popping gunfire had ceased. Wells had no illusions as to which side had won; there were two guards facing off against at least half a dozen intruders. He concentrated on his breathing and climbed the stairs.

It took just over fifteen minutes for Wells to reach the top deck of the tower, but it felt like forever. His chest was on fire, his calf muscles flared in terrible pain with each step taken. Wells brushed the sweaty strands of hair out of his eyes and looked around.

The two guards lay sprawled on the metal floor. Suspended seven feet above the observation deck floor, the iron cage which housed the transmitter was wide open, both of its heavy locks cut off. The transmitter itself was gone.

The crew cut the ropes holding the dirigible to the tower. The airship was rapidly picking up speed as it headed west toward the Seine. It was still close enough for Wells to momentarily lock eyes with one of the crew. The man stared back from the aft of the airship, most of his face covered by a mask.

Wells dove toward one of the guards and wrestled the revolver out of the loosened grip of the unconscious man's hand. He waited several seconds, until the airship was far enough for the impending explosion not to damage the tower. Then he raised the weapon and fired twice at the easy target of the enormous gray balloon keeping the dirigible afloat. He flinched, bracing himself for the shock wave.

Nothing happened.

Wells fired four more times, emptying the cylinder, but the explosion never came. Wells thought that the thieves either figured out a way to inflate the balloon with a gas far less flammable than hydrogen, or they somehow built the dirigible's envelope out of bulletproof gasbags.

His legs finally gave out and Wells slid to the floor. He closed his eyes and tried to regain control of his breathing as he waited for Curie, who had fallen behind, to suffer his way up the stairs.

When the French agent finally arrived, Wells recounted the events of the last few minutes. Curie studied the unconscious guards and panted as he listened to his British counterpart.

Wells stared at the World's Fair grounds below. Finally, he turned to Curie and said: "Sue Ann MacLean is going to kill me."

"YOU'RE MAD," said Doyle. "The greatest security breach in the Ministry's history and you want me to sweep it under the rug, to hide the entire incident from London? MacLean would have both our heads on the plate."

Arthur Conan Doyle was the senior Ministry agent, who recently arrived in Paris for the World Security summit. The clandestine services of all the major world powers sent their representatives to celebrate the success of the joint effort of the Eiffel Tower project and to discuss the possibility of putting the enmity and mistrust that existed between them aside for the benefit of humanity. The heist could not have happened at a worse time.

"Please, Arthur. You know I didn't get assigned to babysitting an architect for two years merely because I drew a short straw. MacLean was punishing me because the mission to Russia didn't work out the way she had intended. And now that the tower is complete and the transmitter was about to go live, I had hoped to get out of Paris and go somewhere interesting for a change. No offense, Pierre," Wells said to Curie, who was frowning into his drink. "I just know MacLean will somehow blame me for what happened, and that will put an end to my career at the Ministry once and for all.

"Please, let me work with the French and the others at the summit. Together we will find the culprits and recover the transmitter expeditiously. All I ask for is a couple of days. If I fail, I shall accept full responsibility and fall on the sword."

Doyle sipped his scotch. "So you think you can solve this mystery, do you?" he asked Wells.

"Yes, with the help of all the agencies. The greatest collection of agents and spies in human history is in Paris now, thanks to the summit. What chance do the hapless robbers have against our combined resources?"

Doyle got up and began pacing back and forth across the small room. "The guards were hit by some sort of a stun weapon," he said. "The attackers were well-trained and efficient operatives who knew about the transmitter, knew how to disconnect it properly, and possessed extraordinary technology. The only organizations I can think of capable of pulling off this heist are the clandestine ministries themselves. The same people you wish to rely upon to help solve this case."

"But why?" asked Curie. "Why would any of them sabotage a project that benefits us all?"

"I don't know," said Doyle. "But if any other group capable of a heist of this magnitude existed anywhere in the world, surely we'd be aware of them. Once you eliminate the impossible, whatever remains, no matter how improbable, must be the truth."

Wells seized on the hypothesis. "Could one of them have allied itself with an outside power, planning exactly the sort of invasion the Eiffel Tower was created to detect? If so, it's all the more reason to collect additional data before reporting any sort of conclusions to London. This is too important to get it wrong."

Doyle continued to pace, the scotch stirring in his glass, small bits of it splashing onto the rug.

"Very well," he said. "I will give you a little time before I report to Ministra MacLean. The summit opens in a few short hours. I have a plan that will allow us to investigate the transmitter heist, and spy on the rival agencies at the same time." Doyle put down the drink and reached for his hat. "Come. We must see a young scientist about her invention."

EACH COUNTRY IN EUROPE, and many beyond, built wondrous exhibits in order to put their best foot forward at the World's Fair. And even though the fair was not yet open to the public, the fairgrounds bustled with activity. National delegations, construction crews, and anyone with some sort of a connection that could gain them early access alternated between putting the finishing touches on their own exhibits and exploring the expositions of others.

The major world powers spared no expense to build

grandiose halls and display national treasures and the latest technologies to wow the attendees. As the host country, France put up the largest exhibit consisting of numerous halls. Wells, Doyle, and Curie walked through the French section, passing the grandiose Hall of Machines and a smaller building heavily guarded by grim, well-armed men. It was the temporary home of the Imperial Diamond – the largest brilliant in the world.

Having cut through the French section and walked farther away from the center of the fairgrounds, they entered into a patchwork of much smaller exhibits set up by the less influential nations. Doyle led them toward a diminutive structure which bore a red coat of arms depicting a crowned white eagle with golden talons and beak.

"Which country is this?" asked Wells.

"Poland," said Doyle.

"Poland?" said Curie. "Half of it is annexed by the Austro-Hungarians and the other half occupied by the Russians. How is it that they even have their own booth?"

"It's politics," said Doyle. "There are many Poles who don't accept the dissolution of the Congress Poland in 1865, and work toward autonomy or even independence. The French aren't overly friendly with the Russians at the moment, and so they found it convenient to allow these nationalists their own exhibit."

The agents were shown inside and escorted into a cramped room in the back. They didn't have to wait long; shortly after they settled into their chairs, a petite blonde woman with blue eyes walked in, carrying a medium-sized suitcase.

The men got up from their seats, and Curie rushed forward and tried to help with her luggage, almost knocking over his chair. The woman waved off the help. She nodded politely to Doyle.

"Gentlemen, meet Maria Sklodowska, an up-and-coming inventor and physicist," said Doyle.

The men introduced themselves. Curie, usually cool and collected, stammered and almost mispronounced his own name.

"Miss Sklodowska and I spoke earlier and she has agreed to help us. She invented a device that will be extremely useful at the summit," said Doyle. "Would you please show them?"

"Remember our deal, Mr. Doyle," said Sklodowska. "I lend you the use of my invention and you get me a position at the science department of the Ministry of Preternatural Affairs."

"You have my word," said Doyle. "Given your splendid mind, it is a wonder MacLean hasn't recruited you already,"

Sklodowska opened the suitcase and retrieved a package wrapped in several layers of cloth. She carefully unfolded the bundle and produced a pair of extra-thick glasses attached by a thin copper wire to a gadget encased in a polished chrome box the size of a notebook.

She proudly held out the contraption, glasses in one hand and the gadget in another. "This machine can analyze heart rate, speech patterns, perspiration, and dozens of other metrics from any person I observe through the attached lenses. The computational engine within studies this information faster than a human being ever could. It's capable of making ten raised to the power of a hundred calculations per day, which is why I named the technology Googol Glasses. I refer to the device as the truth detector, for the benefit of the mathematically challenged."

"You mean to tell us that you are able to determine

whether someone's lying by merely glancing at them through this contraption?" asked Wells.

"It takes a few moments to establish a baseline, but yes. It can determine one's sincerity with amazing accuracy," said Sklodowska.

"Of all the wondrous inventions and mighty weapons of the modern age, this may be the most dangerous I've seen yet," said Doyle. "The princes and magnates of today will not accept lightly the existence of a scientific method for determining their probity."

"You're right, of course," said Curie. "But it certainly serves our immediate needs. We shall interview the members of each agency and see if we can catch any of the clandestine bastards in their lies." Curie paused. "A lie detector. I think I like the sound of that better."

"I think not," said Sklodowska. "It has been my experience that anyone worth examining articulates many more lies than truths. You search for the needle in a haystack, not for the hay surrounding the needle."

"The truth detector it is, then," said Wells. "To be frank, I don't care if you call it Suzie, so long as it helps us recover the transmitter."

After a brief strategy session, the men left the Poland booth.

"What was that, in there?" Wells asked Curie. "I've never seen you so skittish around women before."

"I've never met such a brilliant woman," said Curie. "And she's incredibly beautiful, too." Curie walked in the sort of a happy trance that can only be inflicted by Cupid's arrow. "Do you think she might agree to have dinner with me, after this heist business is over and dealt with?"

THE ENVOYS from the world's top clandestine agencies listened intently as Wells and Curie recounted the events of that morning. A dozen men and women were seated around a long conference table, with the two young agents speaking from the front of the room. Sklodowska was introduced as a secretary who suffered from astigmatism. She sat inconspicuously in the corner, observing the gathering through her lenses and meddling with the device they were attached to.

Count Ferdinand von Zeppelin leaned back, his chair creaking underneath his girth. A thick white mustache dominated his face, appearing even more prominent in contrast with his shaved head. "You can't bring a well-constructed dirigible down with a firearm," he explained. "A shot would pierce the lift bag, but you'd need a spark. In the future, take care to arm the guards with explosive bullets."

While others listened in silence to the description of the heist at the top of the Eiffel Tower, von Zeppelin kept interrupting and peppering Wells with questions about the design and construction of the airship.

"The airbags must have been filled with helium," he said. "The Americans do this; helium is in far greater supply in the New World."

Everyone turned toward a short, thin woman who wore a cowboy hat and rested a pair of long leather boots on the edge of the table.

"My people had nothing to do with this," said Annie Oakley. "It's not like an airship can cross the Atlantic. Whoever the thieves are, they have a European base of operations. And aren't you an expert on dirigibles, chubby?"

She glared at von Zeppelin, whose face turned an interesting shade of red. He opened his mouth to speak, but Oakley waved him off. "Oh, relax, I'm just joshin' you. I'm still sore over my crew losing out to your team in Calcutta." She smiled and turned to Wells. "Besides, if you can't bring an air balloon down with a gun — helium or not — you are not using enough gun."

"Ms. Oakley's theory has merit," said Mori Ogai of Japan. "We must look to agencies with bases within a dirigible's reach."

"Of course you like her theory," grumbled Vincent van Gogh. "It shifts the suspicion away from you. Except that the European agencies have plenty of otherworldly tech to work with. It's the second-rate outfits like yours that must resort to stealing the table scraps, so you can keep up with the big boys."

Everyone spoke out at once, tempers flaring, insults and recriminations flying across the room.

"Enough!" roared Jules Verne. "I will have order." The head of the Deuxième Bureau banged his palm against the table and glared at everyone else until they ceased their squabbling one by one and there was silence in the conference room.

"Don't you see," said Verne once he had everyone's attention, "this must be what the thieves want. To sow discord among the agencies and stomp out the budding spirit of co-operation that has been nurtured by this joint enterprise." Verne leaned on the table with both hands. "We must band together, combine our resources as never before to track down and retrieve the transmitter. Now, then, let's talk about how we can best coordinate our efforts on this."

The meeting went on for nearly an hour.

AFTER EVERYONE ELSE HAD GONE, Wells, Doyle, and Curie eagerly crowded Sklodowska.

"What have you learned?" Wells rubbed his hands together in anticipation. "Which one of them was lying?"

Sklodowska looked uncomfortable. "All of them, at one point or another. Truth does not seem to come easily to people in your line of work. As to the specific question of the heist..." She hesitated for a moment. "I think I would prefer to discuss it with Mr. Doyle alone."

"Nonsense," said Curie. "We are in this together, and we deserve the truth."

"That's right," said Wells. "It's exactly as Verne was saying; we must work together on this."

Sklodowska looked to Doyle, who nodded.

"Very well." She frowned, and then put the Googol Glasses back on. "I insist on asking each of you first, did you have anything to do with this heist?"

Wells frowned. The implied accusation stung, but he understood Sklodowska's need for caution. He affirmed his innocence, and the other two men grudgingly did the same. Sklodowska nodded, satisfied, and removed the glasses.

"Everyone in this room was an accomplished liar," she said, "but only one of them lied about their knowledge or involvement with this theft." Sklodowska turned to Curie. "The reason I wanted to speak to Doyle alone, was because that particular liar was your boss."

"Jules Verne stole the transmitter?" Wells stared at Sklodowska in surprise. He certainly did not anticipate this outcome, and was wondering if perhaps she might be a double agent, feeding them misinformation in order to sow discord between two of the most powerful ministries at the summit.

Curie looked as though he had been hit by lightning. "There must be some sort of a mistake," he stammered. "Messier Verne would never—"

"But he did," Sklodowska cut him off. "He was undoubtedly lying when he suggested the reason for the heist. Verne is holding something back, and I'm sure he knows who took the transmitter, if it wasn't his own people."

Curie raised his index finger and opened his mouth to speak, but after a second's hesitation lowered his hand and dropped into a chair, his shoulders slumped. "Why?" he asked. "Why would Verne do such a thing?"

"It makes sense," said Doyle. "Suppose Verne directs the efforts of all the agents who are here for the summit, and recovers the transmitter after a few days. It will give the black eye to our ministry and the entire British Empire, and allow the French to replace us as de facto leaders of the newly formed coalition of agencies by the time this World's Fair ends."

"That is underhanded and devious," said Wells.

"Yes, and exactly the sort of thing MacLean would do too, if she had thought of it first," said Doyle. "Espionage is a full-contact sport."

Wells rubbed his chin. "Shall we confront Verne in front of the others and expose his scheme?"

"We haven't sufficient evidence and I'm not prepared to expose the existence of Ms. Sklodowska's invention to every agency in the world," said Doyle. "No, we must investigate quietly and recover the transmitter before Verne's people do."

"What about you?" Sklodowska looked at Curie. "You are an agent of the French ministry, so where do your loyalties lie in this?"

Curie chewed his lip and stared off into space as he thought it over. "Verne charged me with protecting the transmitter and then threw me under the horse carriage. I'm loyal to France, and won't commit to any action that will harm my country, but retrieving and activating the transmitter expeditiously will benefit everyone, including my countrymen. So I will help you look for it, Verne's schemes be damned."

Wells gripped Curie's shoulder. He appreciated how difficult his friend's choice must've been. He also wondered if he would possess the courage to make the similar choice, were he in Curie's shoes.

"I believe him," said Sklodowska.

"You're not wearing your truth detector glasses," pointed out Doyle.

Sklodowska gave Curie another appraising look and said, "I know."

WELLS AND HIS TEAM exercised extreme caution as they moved, ever so slowly, down the dark corridor, each step bringing them closer to Jules Verne's office.

Breaking into the heart of hearts of the Deuxième Bureau was reckless, dangerous, and their best chance at discovering what Verne might know about the heist. Curie was clearly uncomfortable with smuggling foreign nationals into the "Second Bureau" – France's top spy agency – but he was committed to helping his allies.

Curie's credentials got him into the building and past the

armed guards in the vestibule. He broke into one of the offices on the ground floor, propped open its window, then helped Doyle, Wells, and Sklodowska climb inside. Getting to the top floor, where Verne's private suite of offices was located, wasn't difficult. The trouble would come next; Curie knew that the top floor contained many booby traps set to defend against such unwelcome intrusions, but wasn't high enough on the Bureau totem pole to possess the knowledge of their nature or locations.

It took nearly fifteen minutes for Doyle to defeat the lock and open the door leading from the staircase onto the top floor – and only after Sklodowska's sharp eye found the very thin copper wire which undoubtedly connected the door to some sort of an alarm. Wells made a careful cut, then stuck the knife into the doorframe and tied the wire to it, maintaining the pressure that would prevent it from setting off whatever nasty surprise the wire connected to.

Once inside, Sklodowska lit a candle. It illuminated a long corridor with rows of doors on each side. Verne's office was behind the heavy oak door directly ahead, at the far end of the hallway.

The four of them edged forward slowly and very quietly, constantly searching for evidence of more security measures. It was only because the building was so quiet that Wells heard a soft click when he stepped onto a section of parquet flooring. "Down," he hissed as the panels on both sides of the corridor began to shift.

Doyle and Wells threw themselves out of the way. Sklodowska hesitated for a fraction of a second but Curie tackled her onto the ground. A dozen darts shot from both directions, sailing a hair's width above Curie's head as he and

Sklodowska tumbled to the floor.

Everyone kept their heads down until they were certain that no more projectiles were flying.

"Get off me, you oaf!" Sklodowska shoved at Curie.

Curie pushed himself from atop Sklodowska, his face burning red. He offered his hand, to help her up, but wouldn't look her directly in the eyes. Sklodowska ignored the proffered hand, got up on her own, and brushed off her dress. Wells and Doyle exchanged a meaningful glance, but made no comment.

Doyle picked up one of the darts, careful to avoid touching the sharp end. He sniffed at it. "Must be some sort of poison or paralyzing agent," he whispered. He studied the open wall panels. "It appears to be a mechanical device. I don't think it set off any alarms."

Wells moved into the lead. "Stay a few steps behind me," he told the others, "and take care to follow precisely in my footsteps."

Wells's heart raced. Each panel he chose to step on was a risk, each step forward without setting an alarm a small victory. He had no way of knowing where the traps were hidden and had to rely on blind luck. He fervently hoped that he was overdue a small measure of good luck.

His luck held out, and the group arrived at Verne's door without setting off any more traps. Doyle reached for his lock picks but they weren't needed – the door wasn't locked.

"Remember the crystal," said Curie softly. He opened the door with great care, moving it as slowly as he could. On the other side, a few steps into the room, stood a small round coffee table with ornate legs. A shimmering yellow crystal the size of an egg rested on its surface.

It was the one security item Curie knew of and had warned the others about in advance. The Second Bureau found the crystal in the jungles of the Philippines, its origins lost in antiquity. The crystal was sensitive to movement. A person walking past it at a leisurely pace prompted a shrill noise louder than the call of a carnival barker. If one ran past the crystal it let out a cry so loud it would be heard all the way across the Seine.

Curie inched toward the crystal as slowly as he could. Even at his snail's pace, the crystal murmured, getting louder as Curie closed in on it. Wells gaped at the ancient artifact. Despite his status as a Ministry agent and ready access the position granted to all sorts of unusual devices, this was the most alien thing he had ever seen.

When Curie finally reached the table, he removed his bowler hat and placed it gently on top of the coffee table, covering the crystal.

"Clear." Curie exhaled with relief, wiped the sweat off his forehead, and motioned for the others to come in.

Verne's office was spacious and the antique shelves along the walls were decorated with many of the curious items his agency had gathered from around the world. Wells resisted the urge to gawk at the moon rock, or the dinosaur bones the Second Bureau had recovered from deep inside a dormant volcano. Instead, he looked for papers or any other evidence of Verne's complicity in the Eiffel Tower heist.

Sklodowska went straight for Verne's desk, expertly picking the locks on its drawers one by one and scanning through the contents. She held up a page. "Oh wow, according to this, Nostradamus was a mechanical assassin from the future, sent back in time to kill—"

"Give me that!" Curie snatched the sheet from Sklodowska's hand. "Sorry," he said. "State secrets, and all that. Kindly stick to the more recent documents." He slid the page back into its place in the drawer.

They searched the desk and the bookshelf behind it, but found no useful evidence until Doyle waved them over to a landscape painting on one of the walls. "There is no dust," he said. "All the other ones had a bit of dust collecting behind the top of their frames. Verne's maid isn't very thorough."

The others crowded behind Doyle and watched him remove the painting from its place on the wall. It revealed the door to a cast iron safe. The handle and the dial of the combination lock protruded from its sleek surface.

"Aha!" Doyle leaned in, his ear touching the safe, and turned the dial.

And the weight of the world came down on their heads.

An enormous force pushed Wells to the ground. It pressed down on him and restricted his movements. He could barely wiggle his fingers and turn his head only slightly, to see that everyone else was pinned down on the floor around him. There was nothing above them, but it felt as though the air itself had turned to lead. Wells cursed under his breath. The Bureau defenses had defeated them after all.

A few minutes later the door opened and Jules Verne walked in. Wells cursed again. Held firmly to the ground, he had time to contemplate how much trouble they were all in.

"What do we have here?" Jules Verne strolled past the immobilized agents, examining each of them in turn as one might study an exotic animal at the zoo. "Three foreign spies and a domestic traitor, killed during a failed assassination attempt." He paused, letting the words sink in. "How very embarrassing this episode will turn out to be for the British Crown." He rubbed his hands gleefully.

"I'm no traitor," shouted Curie, his voice partially muffled by whatever was holding them down. "You're the traitor, stabbing your allies in the back and risking the security of the entire world, and for what – a short-term political gain? You disgust me. Do to us what you will—any fate is better than listening to you gloat."

"Let's not be so hasty," Doyle said quickly. "Give the nice insane villain the chance to lay bare his plans, if he really wants to."

"Very well." Verne was smiling unkindly at his captives. "We have a few minutes before the air inside the force fields that are enveloping each of you runs out. I am told suffocating is a painful and prolonged way to die."

Wells struggled against the invisible restraints, but still couldn't move more than a few inches. Whatever it was Doyle was buying time for, Wells couldn't figure out how to help his friend take advantage of it.

"Before I kill you, Mr. Doyle, I shall indeed take this rare opportunity to gloat. Yes, I intend on embarrassing the British and gaining political advantage, just like young Curie has surmised. But I am also getting paid an enormous sum of money for the few days' use of the transmitter device. More than enough francs to retire in comfort. And now that I have all of you, no one will doubt that this heist was the work of British agents gone rogue, perpetrated by the very people put in charge of protecting the transmitter. So you see, your deaths will serve my cause nicely. In the end, I always win."

"Not quite," said Doyle. "We've heard enough evidence to sink you. Now!" he shouted.

There was the sound of an explosion. The door of Verne's office was blown off its hinges and flew inward, slamming against the antique shelves with incredible force and scattering the prizes Verne had collected around the room. Armed men poured through the opening, lining up against the walls and pointing an array of futuristic and alien weapons at the shocked Verne. Between all of them, the armaments were impressive and varied enough that they could belong to only one ministry in the world.

"Sorry, chap," Doyle said to Wells. "I couldn't keep this sort of an operation secret from our superiors. And besides, I was rather certain we'd need the backup."

One of the Ministry men found and pulled a heavy ivory lever protruding from the wall behind a shelf, and suddenly Wells was able to move once again. He watched his comrades scramble onto their feet; the field that held them in place had been terminated.

With the room secured and Verne held down by a pair of Ministry operatives, a woman in her late fifties walked through the jagged opening that had once been the door.

She wore a flowing black skirt and a high-collared shirt with a military-style red jacket over it. There was a holster on her right hip and a gleaming brass spaulder which housed some sort of otherworldly tech over her right shoulder and arm. Her gray hair was cut very short. Large pearl stud earrings were the only jewelry she wore.

She walked past the subdued Verne as though he wasn't there and came to rest in front of the agents, who tried their best to stand at attention despite their aching muscles.

Sue Ann MacLean, Her Majesty's Ministra of the Preternatural Affairs, turned to Wells and said: "Still getting yourself in trouble, I see?"

She brushed off the excuses Wells attempted to mumble, nodded in turn to each of his friends, and finally turned her attention to Verne. "Where is the transmitter?" she asked.

Verne scowled at her, refusing to talk.

MacLean reached into one of the many pockets on her jacket, took out a small syringe filled with a milky liquid and, before anyone could react, stabbed its needle into Verne's neck. "Truth serum," she said. "Soon he will tell us everything we want to know."

As they waited for the serum to take effect, a group of French agents burst into the room. Colonel Jean Sandherr looked over the ransacked office, his captured boss, and the discarded syringe on the ground.

"This isn't what we agreed to," he told MacLean. "I can't have you drugging the head of the Deuxième Bureau."

"He is guilty," said MacLean. "My people recorded him admitting as much. You can have the evidence." She extended her hand and Doyle handed over a miniature phonograph he had concealed in his pocket.

Sandherr accepted the phonograph and passed it along to one of his men. "If Verne is a traitor, we shall interrogate him ourselves, and inform you of the results."

MacLean advanced on Sandherr and stared him down. "You listen to me," she waved an index finger in his face, "that pathetic excuse of a man stole something that belongs to the Crown, and he did it in the hopes of besmirching my agency's stellar reputation on the world stage.

"If you impede me from doing my job and recovering the transmitter, I shall return the favor in kind and let the entire world know just how badly you people screwed up. And I will keep letting them know this until there is so much opprobrium for your government that people everywhere will henceforth choose to refer to their lunch bread as freedom baguettes."

Sandherr flinched, swallowed hard, and then nodded and stepped out of MacLean's way.

THE CASE OF THE YELLOW SUBMARINE

WELLS CURSED THE FATES, Verne, and especially MacLean, as he navigated his way through the ramshackle shipping docks at the edge of town, along the coast of the Seine. He tried to shake the fog from his head, breathing deeply of the early morning air which smelled of fish and rot and a hint of sulfur.

Wells had managed two hours of sleep before he'd been roused by a messenger. MacLean summoned him to an urgent meeting, but instead of the British embassy, the coachman brought him all the way out here. Wells winced as the river mud splattered his expensive shoes and the bottom of his trousers.

The coachman held the door open and motioned for Wells to step inside a wooden warehouse on the water's edge. It extended a dozen yards into the river, partially covering a pier.

Inside, Wells discovered that a submersible the size of a stagecoach was docked at the pier. Its hull was painted bright yellow. A dozen workers milled around it, welding and tinkering, and causing a loud racket unwelcome by Wells's sleep-deprived brain. MacLean was engaged in an animated discussion with Alfred Nobel, the agency's official armourer. Nobel was valued for his scientific genius and trusted implicitly, despite being a foreigner in the most British of clandestine services.

A few steps away from the Ministra and the armourer stood Arthur Conan Doyle, Pierre Curie, and Maria Sklodowska. All of them looked like they needed rest as much as Wells did, but at least they were drinking coffee. They had somehow procured oversized ceramic mugs that looked almost like steins, not the tiny, dainty porcelain cups favored by the Parisian bakeries. Doyle was kind enough to have one ready and filled for his friend.

Wells gratefully accepted the mug and drank. The coffee was lukewarm and bitter, and just what he needed. "Why are we here?" he asked.

"I think we're about to find out." Doyle nodded at MacLean and Nobel, who were making their way toward the group.

"Good morning," said MacLean. Wells was almost certain that she hadn't slept at all, but she didn't show it. MacLean looked as sharp and intimidating as ever.

MacLean nodded toward the table by the wall that housed a small breakfast spread and Nobel headed over to get her a cup. "We know where the transmitter is. Verne accepted an extra-large bribe in exchange for lending it to an Austrian neurologist named Sigmund Freud."

"The transmitter is in Vienna?" Curie nearly spilled his drink.

Wells knew that the relationship between France and the Austro-Hungarian Empire was already strained, and such a development would only make things more difficult for everyone involved.

MacLean fixed the French agent with a withering gaze until he got the hint that the Ministra didn't appreciate being interrupted. "Verne is an opportunist, but he isn't a fool," she said. "He didn't let the transmitter leave the country. Well, not precisely. Freud wanted to conduct some experiment that requires the alien technology inside the transmitter, so Verne set up a secure base on a small island off the coast of Normandy, where his loyalists are present to keep an eye on both Freud and the transmitter."

Nobel returned and handed MacLean a cup of tea. She was too properly British to consider ingesting any other caffeinated drink in a civilized setting.

She smiled at the armourer and took a sip, the liquid white with an abundance of milk and sugar. "I want the transmitter retrieved and placed back atop the tower by the time the World's Fair opens to the public, and I want this handled quietly. Since the four of you are already aware of the particulars of this case, I would prefer to have you undertake this mission instead of me reading in additional staff.

"Mr. Doyle, Mr. Wells, you have your orders." MacLean looked at Curie. "Agent Curie, you are on loan to us, courtesy of Coloner Sandherr, who's succeeded Verne as the director of the Deuxième Bureau. Understood?"

"What is to happen to Verne?" asked Curie.

"Our governments have jointly decided it was best to avoid a scandal. He will retire from public service and live out the rest of his life quietly." She winced. "Writing adventure books."

MacLean turned her attention to Sklodowska. "Young lady, you're under no obligation to help us whatsoever. Even so, you have proven to be a valuable asset, and I would be glad to have your participation, should you choose to volunteer it."

The two women studied each other briefly. "I don't relish leaving matters unfinished," said Sklodowska. "I'm in."

"You shall travel to the îles Saint-Marcouf via submarine," said MacLean. "It is both expeditious and furtive. The submersible has been loaded with food, maps, and supplies. If you leave now, you will arrive at the shores of île du Large before sunrise tomorrow."

"This beauty is an experimental model. It can navigate the Seine's shallow waters and move fast for its size," said Nobel. "Up to twenty kilometers per hour!"

Everyone turned and looked at the little submarine.

"Why is it yellow?" asked Wells.

Nobel coughed then adjusted his jacket. "The original design had the unfortunate tendency to power down and to sink. The bright exterior makes it easier to find and dredge out from the bottom of the river, you see. But don't worry; I'm almost certain we've since worked all those issues out."

"This is a mistake," Wells said suddenly.

"I assure you, this vessel is shipshape," retorted Nobel.

"Not that," said Wells. "The secrecy, the lies... This summit was supposed to be about fostering the cooperation between the world's clandestine services. Yet here we are, with limited resources and time, and only because we wish to preserve face." He looked MacLean straight in the eye. "If we can't bring ourselves to work with the others on something like this, what chance do we have in uniting against the real threats, in the future?"

Everyone waited for the famous MacLean temper to well up, to explode, but she frowned and took a long, deliberate sip of her tea.

"I appreciate your candor, Mr. Wells," she finally said, "but you have your orders."

"I WAS HOPING it would somehow turn out to be bigger on the inside," said Wells.

The cabin of the submarine was cramped and uncomfortable. It could barely seat the four of them. The agents suffered through a twenty-hour journey, north via the river Seine and then due west in the deeper waters of the English Channel.

Wells managed several catnaps, but he was sore and achy, and eager to disembark. He looked over at Sklodowska, who appeared even less comfortable, shifting in her hard-backed seat.

"Not the glamorous life of a secret agent you imagined, is it?" said Wells.

"I respect what you do," said Sklodowska, "but I don't romanticize it. I have no interest in being a field agent. I just want a job at the Ministry lab."

"Why do you want to work for the Crown, anyway? You aren't British." Wells crossed his hands behind his neck, stretching the arm muscles.

"Aren't you the ones always claiming to work for the benefit of the entire world?" countered Sklodowska. "It's quite simple, really. I'm a scientist. Your ministry has access to the best cutting-edge science out there, so that's where I belong."

"You seem to be doing fine on your own," said Wells, pointing at the suitcase housing the Googol Glasses machine.

"I've grown adept at reverse-engineering otherworldly tech," said Sklodowska. "Can you imagine how different our world would be today if aliens, and time travelers, and inter-dimensional beings hadn't begun showing up with increasing frequency around the time Victoria was crowned queen?

"We could have been great on our own, could have ushered in the age of copper and steam, and sparked the second industrial revolution. I could have studied physics, or chemistry, or engineering, and truly created something original. Instead, we're all reduced to fighting over scraps of somebody else's contraptions. Scavenging parts to put together a gadget like this," she pointed to the suitcase, "is pretty much all a scientist can aspire to these days. There's little sense in trying to invent something new when you know with absolute certainty that there already exist versions of the same technology so advanced, they're practically indistinguishable from magic."

Wells thought it over, trying to imagine the world without the technological wonders. A world without the Ministry. A smaller world. Would an alternate version of him amount to anything in such a place? He didn't much like the idea.

"We should be right here," Doyle pointed at the two dots on the map, well off the coast of Europe. He spread the map out as wide as the tiny cabin would allow while Curie piloted the miniature vessel.

"Well, we aren't," said Curie. "There's nothing around but water and more water. You must be reading the map wrong."

"I'll have you know that I'm a master navigator," said

Doyle. "Perhaps if you were to keep a steadier hand on the ship wheel—"

"Boys, boys," Sklodowska interjected before the argument could escalate. "There is no reason to assign blame. Not when the three of you and your spy games are clearly responsible for me being cooped up in this underwater dinghy with stale air and limited toilet facilities. I'm going to take out my frustration on *somebody*, and you better hope we reach Verne's men before that happens, or my options will be limited to the persons present." She smiled sweetly at her traveling companions.

Curie gripped the wheel tighter. "Just keep looking," he told Doyle.

"I *am* looking. It's not like we can pull over and ask for directions," said Doyle, but he redoubled his efforts.

By the time the yellow submarine emerged at the shore of île du Large, it was almost dawn.

A NUMBER OF SMALL BOATS were grounded on the beach. A larger steamship was anchored in deep water, between île du Large and île de Terre, the smaller of the two Malcouf islands.

A circular fort dominated the center of the island. A moat was dug around it, carving out most of the island grounds in an uneven hexagon. Only patches of rocky beach and some areas of wild grass, beaten down by the strong winds and growing almost parallel to the soil, remained on the outside. The high stone walls surrounding the area on the inside of the moat and the towering fort above them made the structure look like a medieval castle.

"Why do they need a moat on an island surrounded by leagues of ocean water?" asked Sklodowska.

"It must be peer pressure," said Curie. "Every self-respecting villain has to have a moat these days. I was on a mission in Belgium once, where the moat was filled with sharks which had Gatling guns grafted onto their heads."

"How did you get past that?" asked Wells.

"We threw some meat scraps into the water, causing a feeding frenzy, which resulted in a shooting frenzy. Gatling sharks are a terribly inefficient security system."

The agents docked the submarine at a raggedy wooden pier which extended from the shore, connecting to the road that led to the only egress point of the fort. There was nowhere to hide the bright-yellow submersible anyway. They'd have to rely on speed and the element of surprise to accomplish their mission. The four of them disembarked and headed up toward the fort entrance just as the first glimpse of the rising sun painted the Eastern horizon in brighter hues.

"Halt!" A single sentry posted in the guard tower inside the gate rubbed his eyes and peered into the night, trying to decipher the identities of the four strangers who had somehow appeared on the uninhabited island.

"It's me, Pierre," said Curie. "Verne sent us."

The sentry climbed down from his perch above the wall and opened a metal peep hole in the gate. He held up a dim lantern, producing just enough light to make out Curie's facial features.

"What's the password?" asked the sentry.

Wells and Doyle exchanged a glance. The treacherous Verne mentioned nothing about a password, and they knew it would be impossible to guess. Agency protocols required each pass code to be at least eight characters long, and contain both letters and numbers.

"Philippe? Philippe Pétain?" said Curie. "Don't you recognize me? We were on the Ivory Coast mission together."

"Sure, sure," said Pétain, "Yet, the regulations—"

"Of course," Curie interjected smoothly. "But I can't very well say the password in front of my subordinates." He pointed at the rest of the group. "They haven't got the clearance. Let us in. It's nasty and cold out here."

Wells winced, expecting the sentry to demand that Curie whisper the password to him through the peephole. But there must've been a reason this henchman was assigned to overnight duty guarding a gate on an uninhabited island, and Curie seemed to know it. After a few seconds' wait, the door opened and the four agents were admitted inside.

Pétain held the door open as the four of them piled into the guard tower. Pétain followed them in and his eyes grew wide when he recognized the British agents.

Before the sentry had a chance to react, Curie moved closer, and pressed a long, thin dagger against the man's throat. "Screaming would be very bad for your health, friend. Do yourself a favor and hear me out, all right?"

Pétain turned pale, but didn't shout. He nodded very carefully, making sure the blade didn't pierce his skin.

"Verne is no longer in charge, and everyone involved in this mess will be in serious trouble, likely kicked out of the Bureau and possibly arrested." Curie paused, allowing his captive a moment to process the news.

"I was just following orders," said Pétain.

"That's what every one of them is going to say," said Wells. "An excuse that defeated bad guys have fallen back on with remarkable consistency, throughout history. Do you think the judge will not have heard it before?"

Pétain said nothing. He chewed his lip and strained to keep away from the sharp edge of the blade.

"Help us now, and we'll put in a good word," said Curie.

"What do you want me to do?" asked Pétain.

Curie withdrew the blade and nodded to Sklodowska, who put on her Googol Glasses. "Where is the transmitter?"

"Inside." Pétain pointed toward the round building at the center of the island. "Freud has it hooked up to some sort of strange contraption he built. It's ready to go; they were just waiting for the last of the children to arrive."

"Children?" Wells leaned in, fists clenched.

"Freud said he won't hurt them!" Pétain raised his palms.

"He's experimenting on *children*? What sort of an experiment? What is Freud doing here?" Wells was ready to punch the sniveling guard. Doyle put his hand firmly on Wells's shoulder to hold him back.

"All I know is that Freud claims his machine can turn people into super-soldiers. He needed the alien tech in the transmitter to help make it work, and he brought in a half dozen young children because he said his invention doesn't work on the brain chemistry of adults." Pétain spoke rapidly, and kept a wary eye on Wells.

"Where are they?" Wells growled.

"Everybody but me is inside the fort," said Pétain.

Doyle produced a sheet of paper and a pencil. "Draw us a map."

THE AGENTS LEFT the hapless guard tied up in the tower. He may have switched his allegiance based on the news they shared, but he hadn't earned their trust.

Armed with Pétain's crude schematic of the fort, the four of them slipped into the large circular structure. Designed as the barracks for the French troops in the early 1800s, the building was capable of housing up to 500 people. There were plenty of rooms on the ground level as well as a staircase leading to several more underground. Everyone must have been still asleep – the agents traversed the empty hall and followed Pétain's directions to the room which housed Freud's lab.

The machine inside was enormous. Brass tubes connected a mish-mash of large gear blocks, powered alternatively by steam, electrical current, and energies so obviously foreign to this world that Wells felt the twinges of a headache developing each time he would spend more than a moment or two staring at those components.

There was a round metal platform placed in the center of the lab two steps above floor level. A rifle-like barrel was suspended at an angle above the platform, aimed squarely at its center. And attached to the oblong module that connected the barrel to all the other parts spread across the room was the transmitter.

"This is spectacular," said Sklodowska. She raced around the room, studying the components and touching the tubes that connected them, her irises wide.

"What does this monstrosity do?" asked Doyle.

"I have no idea," said Sklodowska as she crouched to examine an array of dials built into one of the panels, "but the way it melds human and otherworldly technologies is more advanced than anything I have ever seen."

Curie shrugged. "You've seen one mad scientist's lair, you've seen them all."

"You have no appreciation for science," said Sklodowska.

"There's no time for bickering," said Doyle. He pulled up a stool, climbed atop it, and began to unscrew the large bolts connecting the transmitter to the module.

"Wait," said Sklodowska. "What about the children?"

Doyle paused. He gripped the transmitter so tight that his knuckles began turning white. Wells knew Doyle well enough to understand the sort of emotional struggle playing out in his mind, even if his face remained calm.

"We're here to complete the mission," said Doyle. "This Doctor Freud won't have cause to harm the little ones, not if we render his lab inoperable." He resumed untwisting the bolts.

"There are innocent children being held captive in this building, away from their families, and probably terrified. Life as a spy may have made you immune to such plight, but I haven't been hanging around secret agents long enough to lose my humanity." Sklodowska stared at each of the three men in turn. "I'm not leaving here without those kids. Who's with me?"

"She's right," said Wells. "How can we claim to protect humanity if we value the success of our mission above the safety of children?"

Curie nodded, and moved over to stand next to Sklodowska.

"Very well," said Doyle. "Go and find them while I dislodge our property from this gaudy collection of scrap metal. Meet me back at the submarine."

Doyle grunted as he redoubled his efforts to unscrew the bolts without a wrench.

Wells, Curie, and Sklodowska descended the stairs to where

Pétain indicated the children were being kept. The chambers on the lower level must have been prison cells. Each had a thick wooden door with an observation window covered with metal bars.

There were muffled noises coming from inside one of the cells. The agents proceeded with caution, peeking in through the security window.

The children were awake, and there was no sign of a guard. Most of the prison cell floor was covered with a row of six low-lying cots. Some dolls and wooden cubes were scattered on the ground, largely ignored by the children.

Five of them were very young, three boys and two girls who looked to be of kindergarten age. Some sat on their cots and others roamed the room, making half-hearted attempts at play. There was no laughter or horseplay. The children seemed defeated, as though they had been robbed of the wonder and curiosity that is the hallmark of youth. The sixth boy was older, perhaps ten. He stretched out on a cot, his feet dangling off. All the children were scrawny and none appeared particularly athletic.

"These are the future super-soldiers?" whispered Wells.

"I think that one just ate his own booger," said Curie.

Sklodowska frowned at the two men and turned the handle. The door creaked in protest as it opened wide. Six pairs of eyes turned toward her.

"Hush." Sklodowska raised a finger to her lips. "It's going to be okay. We're here to get you out."

The kids all spoke at once, with blatant disregard for Sklodowska's plea for silence, and in a variety of different languages. A little boy who was clutching a threadbare blanket stared at Wells for a long moment and then wailed at a volume far exceeding what one might have expected from his diminutive form. Sklodowska rushed toward the crying child with the two agents in tow, but their rapid advance resulted in several of the other kids joining the chorus.

The trio did what they could to calm the children down. Wells felt they were on the verge of success when their efforts were interrupted by a squad of underdressed yet heavily armed men at the door.

WELLS SAT on one of the small cots and did his best to ignore the pandemonium of a half dozen small children flitting across the small room around him. He felt terrible. The Paris assignment was an undeserved punishment for his failure to deliver functioning weather machine technology from the Russian Empire. He accepted the dead-end assignment without complaint and spent two years overseeing construction, and running interference with detractors as Eiffel and his company built the enormous eyesore of an antenna in the heart of Paris. He was doing well, and was certain Sue Ann MacLean would recognize his accomplishments and send him on real missions, full of adventure and excitement, after the World's Fair ended. And then everything went to hell.

In the last forty-eight hours the space transmitter was stolen right in front of him, he had to be rescued by MacLean herself from the stasis trap in Verne's office, and was now once again captured by the bad guys. Verne's men frisked Wells and his companions, confiscating weapons and gadgets, and then simply left them there, locked in the same room with the children they had intended to rescue.

Wells sighed. With this sort of track record, MacLean could

hardly be expected to let him serve porridge in the Ministry cafeteria, let alone become involved in real spy craft again. Assuming he survived the visit to this accursed island at all. He watched Curie and Sklodowska, talking quietly in the corner of the room and sitting a little closer together than was strictly proper.

It was nearly an hour after their capture that the doors opened again. A man in his thirties swaggered in, surrounded by armed goons.

He wore an immaculate gray three-piece suit. Diamond-studded cufflinks glinted from under the sleeves of his jacket, fastening a perfectly starched white shirt. A thick lit cigar dangled from the corner of his mouth. He cocked his head as he examined the agents, one by one.

He puffed a ring of smoke and held the cigar between his index and middle fingers. "So this is what the finest clandestine services in all of Europe send to thwart me? A motley band of bumbling amateurs. It's no wonder you failed; let those who underestimate Sigmund Freud do so at their own peril."

Wells jumped up but the goons prevented him from approaching their leader. "How dare you besmirch us, Freud? Your insults hold no sting, coming from a thief and a kidnapper. Did you gather these tots by luring them into a windowless stagecoach with a promise of candy?"

Freud bellowed a hearty laugh. "Kidnap them? Their parents begged me to treat them. They've been carefully selected for a clinical trial from hundreds of qualified applicants."

"Their parents wanted you to zap them with rays and turn them into super soldiers?" Wells snorted. "A likely story."

"Soldiers?" Freud raised an eyebrow. "You don't even understand why we're here. What need do I have of soldiers? Future wars will be fought by tanks and automatons, not men with bayonets. The conflicts of the twentieth century won't be won with super soldiers, but super generals.

"These children are developmentally delayed. My machine can treat them. It can alter their brain chemistry and change their lives for the better. They could be gifted rather than dim! And once they possess the intellectual capacity to decide such things, I hope they will be grateful enough to accept me as a father figure and let me train them." Freud stepped forward and patted the head of the oldest child, who was drooling as he stared off into space. "When Al grows up, we shall rule Europe as father and son!"

"Super-smart teenage military commanders? There's something to this…" Curie scratched his chin. He was promptly elbowed by Sklodowska.

"You can justify yourself to us all you want," said Wells. "It won't change the fact that you're insane."

"I wouldn't waste my time seeking your approval," said Freud. "I do, however, need to get rid of your compatriot who locked himself in my lab and is threatening to blow it up should anyone attempt to go in."

"Ha! Go, Arthur!" Sklodowska pumped her fist.

"Why would we ever help you?" asked Wells.

"Who said anything about asking for your help? You're leverage." Freud snapped his fingers. "Bring them," he told his men. "Kids, too."

PRODDED BY FREUD'S MEN, Wells and the others ascended the stairs and walked to the barred entrance into the lab.

"Arthur, is it?" Freud shouted at the door. "I have your friends. Open the door and leave the equipment be, and all of you get to live. Otherwise..." He held out his hand to the nearest subordinate until the other man handed him a pistol. Freud tested its weight in his hand and pointed it at Sklodowska. "I think I will shoot the girl, first. You have one minute."

Gun pointed squarely at the scientist, Freud withdrew a pocket watch with his other hand and waited for the seconds to tick off.

"He won't do it," said Wells, injecting as much confidence into his voice as he could muster. "Could you be any more of a stereotypical villain? You're a handlebar mustache away from being an operetta character."

"Say what you will," said Freud past the cigar clenched between his teeth, "but unlike fictional characters I'm not prone to long-winded speeches. Also, I don't bluff." He put away his watch and cocked the hammer on the pistol.

Curie moved in front of Sklodowska, shielding her. "You will have to shoot me first," he told Freud.

"Very well," said Freud and pulled the trigger.

The sound of the shot rang through the fort. Hit at almost point-blank range, Curie grunted and collapsed onto the ground. Sklodowska screamed and grabbed at his torso, propping him up in her arms. A dark red stain was spreading quickly just below his right shoulder.

Startled by the loud noise, several of the children began to cry.

"That's one," said Freud, his voice perfectly calm, as though he were discussing the weather. He retrieved the watch. "Fifteen seconds this time."

For a long moment, everyone but the crying children was silent. Then Doyle shouted from behind the door, "Stop. I'm coming out." There was a sound of a lock being turned and Doyle stepped through, his arms raised.

Freud nodded and handed the gun to the nearest henchman. He peeked inside the lab. "Where's the transmitter?" he asked Doyle.

"It's on the counter," said Doyle, his eyes on Curie's wound.

Freud took another puff of his cigar and looked over the lab. "Why don't you go ahead and reattach it," he told Doyle. "Just in case you set up any… complications."

If looks could kill, Doyle would have incinerated Freud on the spot. He said nothing but headed back into the lab and got to work.

Sklodowska ministered to Curie as best she could. She removed his jacket and used it to stem the flow of blood. "He needs medical attention," she told Freud. "Help him! You said everybody would live."

"I'm not that kind of doctor," said Freud. But he nodded to one of his men, who ran down the hall and returned with a medicine bag. The bullet missed vital organs, which was little consolation to Curie as he winced in pain on the floor, his head in Sklodowska's lap. The henchman crouched over Curie, and began ministering to the wound.

Doyle finished reaffixing the transmitter to the rest of the machinery and stepped back. Freud walked into the lab and motioned for the others to follow. Most of the henchmen filed in behind him, prodding Wells along. A few remained to watch over Sklodowska and Curie.

Freud examined the various modules closely. "It does not

appear to have been sabotaged. And yet, how can I trust you to have resisted meddling with my machine while you were locked in here?" Freud beckoned to the tallest of the children. "Al, why don't you come and stand right over here, there's a good boy."

The gangly ten-year-old stepped onto the elevated platform. There was a goofy grin on his face as he stared into the barrel of the transmitter-enhanced ray gun aimed at him from above.

"If you did leave a nasty surprise, now would be the time to speak up," Freud told Doyle. "You wouldn't want to jeopardize the well-being of this child, would you?"

Doyle stared down Freud with utter loathing, but remained silent. Freud shrugged, and nodded to one of his men, who pulled a lever. The machine sprung to life all around them, strange energies buzzing in thick glass tubes, steam pumping through brass pipes, steel gears picking up speed as they turned.

The barrel-shaped module that was suspended at a forty-five degree angle and aimed at the circular panel on the ground emitted a high-pitched noise and began to shake. Al appeared mesmerized by its barrel, his mouth slightly agape. The idea to move out of its line of fire didn't seem to occur to him.

The noise reached its crescendo and a jagged lightning bolt shot from the module, enveloping Al in a cocoon of crackling energy. Having discharged the bolt, the machine died, filling the room with smoke and a smell of burning rubber.

"I knew it!" Freud advanced on Doyle. "What did you do?"

"I did nothing at all. Whatever design flaw had caused this malfunction is your own fault," said Doyle.

Freud rushed over to Al and grabbed him by the shirt. "How do you calculate the circumference of a circle?"

Al appeared mostly unharmed, except for his hair, which turned bleach white and stuck out wildly in every direction. He stared at Freud without a glimmer of comprehension.

"He isn't a genius," Freud let go of the child's shirt. "He doesn't even comprehend the concept of Pi."

"Mmmm, pie…" said Al.

Freud threw his cigar on the ground and stomped on it in frustration. "I was so sure it would work. All the calculations were perfect, and the transmitter was supposed to enhance and refine the ray…" He trailed off, shoulders slumped. "And what is that noise?"

The sound of a steam engine was coming from outside the fort, and getting louder. Everyone rushed toward the windows. A gargantuan dirigible was approaching the island from the south, at an incredible speed. As it reached the fort, Wells recognized the unique engineering of Count von Zeppelin.

The airship reached the island, flew over the moat, and began its descent onto the courtyard in front of the fort. Some trigger-happy henchman fired at the approaching behemoth. Annie Oakley leaned over the side of the gondola, a savage grin on her face and two very large guns in her hands. She opened fire on the fort, each bullet exploding with the force of a small hand grenade. She devastated the array of cannons at the top of the fort and kept Verne's men suppressed until the dirigible completed its descent.

Sue Ann MacLean jumped out of the gondola the moment the airship touched the ground. She raced toward the fort, followed by Annie Oakley, Mori Ogai, and a half-dozen other agents from around the world.

A few of Verne's men were brave or foolish enough to stand up to the onslaught. They fired at the advancing agents, but MacLean's spaulder emitted a one-way force shield in front of the entire group which deflected incoming bullets with ease, yet didn't prevent the agents from firing an array of projectile, laser, and pulse weapons at the defenders. The fight was over almost before it began.

When MacLean and her team reached the lab, Freud put up no resistance. "I was so certain. I checked the calculations three times. It should have worked," he kept saying as he was led away.

With the cleanup well in hand, and her people tending to the children, rounding up prisoners, and providing Curie with medical attention, MacLean beckoned Wells over, away from the others. He steeled himself for the epic chewing-out to come.

"Thank you, Agent Wells," said MacLean.

"Um. What?" Wells stared, shocked, at his boss.

"All the things you said about cooperation between agencies, about us needing to work together – you were right." MacLean shuffled from foot to foot, unaccustomed to admitting fault. "I spent some time thinking about it and decided to follow your advice. I called a meeting and told the representatives of the other agencies everything. We pooled our resources and worked together to take down Freud.

"This is how it's going to be from now on," said MacLean, "Britain and France, Russia and China, America and the Ottoman Empire – everyone setting aside their politics to unite against common threats. The twentieth century truly is when everything changes. We're going to be ready."

Wells nodded in relief. His own future was looking a little brighter, too.

"Come." MacLean walked over to Sklodowska with Wells in tow.

"Doyle tells me you've conducted yourself very well, young lady," said MacLean. "I'd be honored to employ you as one of my agents."

"Thank you," said Sklodowska, "but I think I'm going to stay in Paris for a while. Pierre is going to need someone to look after him while he recovers." She looked over to where a doctor was bandaging Curie's wound. "He may be an obnoxious boor, but he took a bullet for me."

"I knew you couldn't resist my charms for long," Curie called out.

Sklodowska snorted. "You see? A boor. I will stay only long enough to see him recover. After that, if I never see his smug face again, it will be too soon."

Wells leaned against the wall. With the danger gone and adrenaline draining from his body, he felt very tired.

"Go on," said MacLean. "You deserve to rest. Go find a bed. It will be a while until we sort everything out. My first priority is to get these children back to their parents."

Wells stifled a yawn and headed off in search of an unoccupied room. He caught the eye of Al, who towered over the other children, his wild hair making him seem even taller. Wells waved at him.

The young Albert Einstein waved back.

THE END

AFTERWORD

THE WORLD of *H. G. Wells, Secret Agent* came to exist because I was asked to contribute a story to a steampunk anthology. I was eager to play, but I also knew my limitations. I'm no expert on Victorian-era England. Whatever I wrote, there would be a high likelihood of people pointing fingers and shouting: "He doesn't know what he's talking about. The whalebone corset wasn't even invented until eighteen-something-something!"

I could study up on the Victorians, but I chose to be lazy and write an alternate history yarn instead.

Also, I knew this would have to be a comedy. It's what I know how to write best and I thought it would make the story stand out, since there isn't all that much steampunk humor out there. So, now we have alternate-history steampunk humor as a genre. No matter what, this one would sure be different.

Then I hit upon the idea of making H. G. Wells, an author

I greatly admire and grew up reading, my protagonist. He was to be a Victorian-era James Bond, having adventures around the world instead of writing books. This is alternate history after all, and I can do that.

Once I established the protagonist, I got to thinking: what other well-known historical figures might he meet? As I ventured deeper and deeper down the rabbit hole of research, I realized just how many fascinating writers, scientists, and other larger-than-life individuals were around and available for me to play with in the late nineteenth century.

Remember how I said I was lazy and didn't want to study up on Victorian England? *Mea culpa.* I ended up spending more time on research than writing the damn thing, after all.

I decided that every single named character in the story would be based upon a real person: from the main heroes and villains down to the lowest gate guard. If you encounter a name you aren't familiar with as you read, run a web search and you'll find out who that character is.

A single huge exception to this rule is Sue Ann MacLean. She's the only character in this book not based on someone you can readily Google. There are Reasons for that, Reasons I don't want to reveal just yet. You'll find out more about her in future Wells stories.

The anthology I was invited to never came together, but I had a fun universe to explore and I just kept writing until a short story turned into a novelette, and then into a novella. I have plans for future Wells stories: you'll get to find out how van Gogh really lost his ear, Annie Oakley will blow up more stuff, and the Ministry will become tangled up in the War of Currents between Tesla and Edison.

I loaded this novella to the gills with Easter eggs: from

cheesy pop culture references to little-known historical facts, to direct quotes from the real-world versions of my characters, spoken as dialog. It became a game among my first readers to identify all of these Easter eggs, so I thought it would be fun to include some annotations below, for anyone looking to play "spot the reference."

ALEX SHVARTSMAN

ANNOTATIONS

THE CASE OF THE WEATHER MACHINE

SCENE 1

Armorial Hall of the Winter Palace

The Winter Palace, located in St. Petersburg, was the official residence of the Russian tsars, from 1732 to 1917. The lavishly decorated Armorial Hall served as the event space for many ceremonies.

All of it created a storybook atmosphere the likes of which the young Englishman could only dream of until a few months ago.

Herbert George Wells, a prolific British author, was born in 1866. The opening scene takes place in 1887.

Improbably, the woman from the future had called this gadget "the Babel fish," despite its apparent lack of any ichthyic qualities.

A reference to Douglas Adams's *The Hitchhiker's Guide to the Galaxy*, where the Babel fish universal translator device was an actual fish. The BabelFish.com web site is also named after this fictitious device.

My name is Nikolai Bunge, Chairman of the Cabinet of Ministers.

A noted Russian economist and statesman, Bunge was Chairman of the Cabinet of Ministers, the highest civil administration post in the Russian empire. He rose to this post in 1887 after serving as Finance Minister for five years. Bunge was known as a reformer, introducing many capitalist ideas, overhauling the

Russian banking system, and modernizing the economy. Many of his policies were considered highly protectionist, which makes him a good foil for Wells in this story.

Modern science has proven that there's far more to the world than was previously dreamt of in our philosophy.

A take on Shakespeare's famous line from Hamlet: "There are more things in heaven and earth, Horatio, than are dreamt of in your philosophy." Wells is apparently fond of this line as he references it again at the beginning of the Dirigible Heist case.

Queen Victoria created the Ministry to arm the human race against the future. Twentieth century is when everything changes. And we've got to be ready.

Since the Ministry is so similar in concept to Torchwood (a government agency originally introduced on *Dr. Who*, which was eventually featured on its own spinoff TV show), I thought it amusing to have Wells recite the lines spoken in the opening sequence of the show, adjusting for the century: "Torchwood: outside the government, beyond the police. Tracking down alien life on Earth, arming the human race against the future. The twenty-first century is when everything changes. And you've got to be ready."

We know that Russia has a secret weapon capable of altering weather patterns.

The two greatest wars fought against invaders on Russian soil were the war of 1812 against Napoleon, and World War II. In both cases, Russian defense benefited greatly from the enemy troops, unaccustomed to such cold conditions, becoming mired in harsh Russian winter. It could be argued that in each case the outcome of the wars might have been different had those winters been milder.

SCENE 2

"This mixture is my own invention; I'm going to patent it when I think of a good name. Make sure it's stirred, not shaken. Wouldn't want the drink to be weak."

He turned toward the blonde and flashed his best smile. "My name is Wells. Herbert Wells."

I couldn't have Wells order a martini, because it hadn't been invented yet. Conveniently, Ian Fleming helped me out. In *Casino Royale*, James Bond orders a Vesper martini, a variant on the cocktail that he had invented. Bond says: "The drink's my own invention. I'm going to patent it when I can think of a good name."

Another interesting trope I got to play with is Bond's preference for "shaken, not stirred." Some folks believe this to be a bad idea. In an episode of *West Wing*, President Bartlet rants: "Shaken, not stirred, will get you cold water with a dash of gin and dry vermouth. The reason you stir it with a special spoon is so not to chip the ice. James is ordering a weak martini and being snooty about it."

Things really weren't working out in the way he had imagined. He waited for his drink, composing excuses for Ministra MacLean in his head.

Ministra is not a British title. It's a Latin word for a female minister, currently used in Italian, Spanish, Portuguese, and Latvian. Although it's not mentioned directly in the story, MacLean had adopted the title for her own, once she achieved a Minister-level post as the director of the Ministry of Preternatural Affairs.

"You should have added lemon to that. I take a slice whenever I have to drink Cognac. Makes the vile stuff taste almost tolerable."
Wells looked up at the man advising him, and swallowed the biting remark he was about to make. Standing in front of him was the heir to the Russian throne.

Nicholas Romanov, the last tsar of Russia (still an heir to the throne in 1887) was indeed known for his dislike of Cognac. He occasionally had to drink it at formal occasions and added lemon to temper the taste.

The Ministry's chief had somehow acquired a copy of "The Chronic Argonauts," a short story about traveling through time, which Wells was shopping around to newspaper publishers.

This short story by Wells was published in 1888, seven years before *The Time Machine.*

"Our true nationality is mankind."

Whenever possible, I've tried to use the characters' own words in dialog. The above is an actual quote by H. G. Wells.

SCENE 3

"The tsarevich *wants me to find the leaders of a radical socialist group called the People's Will," said Wells. "They have waged war against the Romanovs for years. In '81 they had quite a coup, managing to assassinate Nicholas's grandfather, Tsar Alexander II."*

The People's Will really existed, and the above statement is historically factual, as is all of the historical information relayed by Wells in his conversation with Doyle.

SCENE 4

"Democracy is the road to socialism."

This quote is attributed to Karl Marx, though there's some dispute as to whether he ever wrote/said these exact words. Wells himself had strong socialist leanings, and so having him "pretend" to be a Marxist was not a great stretch.

"The cause of socialism is a global one."

This one is, supposedly, a Lenin quote, though I can't find the reference via web search. It was often quoted as part of Communist propaganda which I got to experience firsthand, growing up in the Soviet Union in 1980s.

SCENE 5

There was a hunting rifle hanging on the wall.

There's a dramatic principle called "Chekhov's gun." He wrote: "Remove everything that has no relevance to the story. If you say in the first chapter that there is a rifle hanging on the wall, in the second or third chapter it absolutely must go off. If it's not going to be fired, it shouldn't be hanging there."

So I thought it would be fun to have a rifle hanging on the wall of Chekhov's apartment. And to never mention it again for the rest of the story.

"Medicine is my lawful wife and literature is my mistress; when I get tired of one, I spend the night with the other."

An actual Chekhov quote. He was indeed a doctor who became a newspaper columnist, and wrote his plays and short stories on the side.

"Every person lives his real, most interesting life under the cover of secrecy."

Another real Chekhov quote.

"We can place your plays and stories in front of all the right people. By this time next year you could be an award-winning author."

Chekhov did indeed win the Pushkin Prize in 1887 for his short story collection *At Dusk*.

"The Ministry has worked diligently over the years to strike all mentions of the undead from books such as Pride and Prejudice.*"*

A nod to Seth Grahame-Smith's *Pride and Prejudice and Zombies*, wherein he combined the classic Jane Austen novel with elements of modern zombie fiction.

SCENE 6

"Aleksandr Ulyanov, at your service."

Aleksandr Ulyanov was Vladimir Lenin's older brother. In 1887 he was arrested and eventually executed for his part in an assassination plot against Tsar Alexander III. He was the chemist who was preparing bombs the revolutionaries were to throw at Alexander's carriage.

His execution may have played a role in Lenin's increased involvement with the socialist movement.

SCENE 7

"Don't panic!"

Another reference to Douglas Adams's *The Hitchhiker's Guide to the Galaxy*.

SCENE 8

"We're being attacked by invisible men!"

I thought it appropriate for H. G. Wells to face threats reminiscent of his most famous works. *The Invisible Man* is one of his best-known novels, and the plot of the two subsequent cases borrows a few details from *The Island of Dr. Moreau.*

Chekhov grabbed for a crystal vase and shattered it on the floor. "They're barefoot!" he shouted.

Wells nodded and edged closer to the broken glass, pulling the prince along.

This scene was loosely inspired by one of my favorite Chekhov quotes: "Don't tell me the moon is shining; show me the glint of light on broken glass." This is the progenitor of the ubiquitous "show, don't tell" writing advice. And while the line itself didn't fit the plot, I had Anton take advantage of broken glass here, and mentioned moonlight in the scene where he first makes an appearance.

"Rebel scum. The house of Romanov has ruled Russia for nearly three hundred years, and will surely continue to do so for three hundred more. It'll take far more than their parlor tricks to take down the future tsar."

First, I couldn't resist a tiny *Star Wars* reference with "rebel scum." Second, for all of Romanov's confidence, his family's reign came to an end in 1917. Tsar Nicholas II was forced to abdicate in the wake of the February Revolution. His entire family lived under house arrest, until they were ultimately executed by the Bolsheviks in July of 1918.

SCENE 9

"Nightingale recently retired, Stoker and Wilde are entirely consumed by a melodramatic rivalry over some woman, and Kipling is on a long-term mission in India."

The most fun part of writing this series was figuring out which historical personages fit the timetable and could be presented as either Ministry agents or bad guys. In this sentence, I got to play with some off-screen characters. Florence Nightingale would have made an awesome agent but she was sixty-seven years old in 1887. Rudyard Kipling was in India at the time. And there really was a romantic triangle, with both Oscar Wilde and Bram Stoker vying for the hand of Florence Balcombe. She ultimately chose Stoker and the two married in 1878, so the timeline doesn't quite fit in this case, but it was too juicy a coincidence to discard and this is, after all, alternate history.

"You're to oversee the giant space transceiver which Gustave Eiffel is building for us in Paris. This should keep you out of trouble for a few years."

The construction of the Eiffel Tower was approved by the French government in 1886 and the contract with Gustave Eiffel was signed in early 1887. He was to build the structure in time for the 1889 World's Fair, creating a nice segue into the next Wells adventure. The Eiffel Tower remained the world's tallest man-made structure until the completion of the Chrysler Building in 1930.

"In my estimation, the Tunguska weather machine will blow itself up in the next twenty or so years."

I've intentionally remained vague on the precise location of the weather machine, offering only the subtle hints of its placement in Siberia so as not to spoil the reveal. There was a huge explosion there in 1908, referred to as the Tunguska event. Based on the crater size, it is considered to be the largest asteroid or comet impact event on Earth in recorded history.

Of course, it could also have been an enormous, two-century-old steampunk weather machine finally succumbing to its design flaw.

THE CASE OF THE DIRIGIBLE HEIST

SCENE 1

"Mr. Wells, meet the representatives of the Committee of Three Hundred," said Curie. "Monsieurs de Maupassant, Gounod, and Bouguereau."

Many of France's elite, especially those involved in the arts, were opposed to the construction of the Eiffel Tower. When construction began, a Committee of Three Hundred was formed: one member for every meter of the tower's height. De Maupassant, Gounod and Bouguereau were all members of this group, led by a notable architect Charles Garnier.

"In fact, I do not mind the excursion at all. This is presently my favorite place in all of Paris."
"It is?" Gounod asked incredulously.

"The base of this structure remains the one place where I can still enjoy the view of my favorite city without seeing the giddy, ridiculous tower dominating its skyline like a gigantic black smokestack."

After the Eiffel Tower was completed, it is said that Guy de Maupassant often ate lunch in the restaurant at the tower's base. When asked about this, he replied that it was the only place in Paris where the tower was not visible. "The giddy, ridiculous tower dominating Paris like a gigantic black smokestack" is a line lifted directly from the petition by the Committee of Three Hundred, published in a Parisian newspaper in 1887.

...pressure the French government into scrapping the tower after Eiffel's license ran out, in twenty years.

Originally the Eiffel Tower was only supposed to stand for twenty years and be scrapped in 1909, after Eiffel's license had expired and the ownership reverted to the city of Paris.

"This enormous edifice was created to serve as what's called an antenna," said Wells. *"A brand new technology developed by Dr. Heinrich Hertz in recent years, to transmit sound across great distances."*

The first antennas were built in 1888 by Heinrich Hertz, fitting nicely into the timeline of the story.

"To me, tolerating one ugly structure is preferable to the idea of Martian tripods marching down the Champs-Élysées."

Evoking Wells's own *War of the Worlds* here.

France has its own secret agency. The Deuxième Bureau…

The *Deuxième Bureau de l'État-major general* (Second Bureau of the General Staff) was France's military intelligence agency from 1871 to 1940. Even though it has dissolved, "Deuxième Bureau" remains a popular culture generic term for France's intelligence services.

SCENE 2

"Once you eliminate the impossible, whatever remains, no matter how improbable, must be the truth."

A direct quote by Arthur Conan Doyle, variants of which are oft repeated by Sherlock Holmes, his most famous creation.

SCENE 3

"Gentlemen, meet Maria Sklodowska, an up-and-coming inventor and physicist."

While virtually all of the other famous persons mentioned in this chapter really attended the 1889 World's Fair, Maria Sklodowska did not arrive in Paris until several years later. Most of us know her by her French name and her eventual husband's surname: Marie Curie.

It's capable of making ten raised to the power of a hundred calculations per day, which is why I named the technology Googol Glasses.

A Googol is a number equal to ten to the 100th power. Google is named after it, and the device name is, of course, a parody on Google Glass.

Despite my best efforts, I had fallen prey to an unintended anachronism here. The term Googol was not coined until 1902.

Scene 4

"The airbags must have been filled with helium," he said. "The Americans do this; helium is in far greater supply in the New World."

This is historically accurate. In the nineteenth century, the envelopes of European dirigibles were filled with hydrogen, as non-flammable helium was not as widely available as it was in America.

Scene 6

Wells resisted the urge to gawk at the moon rock, or the dinosaur bones the Second Bureau had recovered from deep inside a dormant volcano.

References to Jules Verne's science fiction novels, *Journey to the Center of the Earth* and *From the Earth to the Moon.*

"...Nostradamus was a mechanical assassin from the future, sent back in time to kill—"

A gratuitous nod to the Terminator franchise. Curie doesn't let Sklodowska finish reading the paper because I thought it would be more fun to leave the robo-Nostradamus's target ambiguous.

"Before I kill you, Mr. Doyle…"

Another homage to James Bond.

Colonel Jean Sandherr looked over the ransacked office, his captured boss, and the discarded syringe on the ground.

Colonel Jean Sandherr was, in fact, the director of the real Deuxième Bureau between 1886 and 1895.

"…until there is so much contempt for your government that people everywhere will henceforth refer to their lunch bread as freedom baguettes."

Playing off the 2003 incident when the scandalized American politicians renamed French fries served in the Congressional cafeterias into freedom fries after France refused to support the invasion of Iraq.

THE CASE OF THE YELLOW SUBMARINE

SCENE 1

Its hull was painted bright yellow.

When satirizing British culture one would be remiss not to include The Beatles.

"You shall travel to the îles Saint-Marcouf via submarine."

These are a pair of uninhabited islands off the coast of France in the English Channel. The smaller of the two islands, île de Terre, is unremarkable. However, the larger island, île du Large, is home to a circular fort, surrounded by a moat.

Yes, that's right, a moat. In the middle of nowhere, and separated from the ocean by a tiny strip of sand.

The construction of this fort began on Napoleon's orders in 1803 and completed by 1812. It could accommodate up to 500 troops and included seven underground chambers and a cistern.

And while it may have had a perfectly reasonable historical explanation, this thing looks more like a villain's lair than any other real-life locale I know of.

SCENE 2

"I was hoping it would somehow turn out to be bigger on the inside."

And there's your obligatory *Dr. Who* reference.

"There's little sense in trying to invent something new when you know with absolute certainty that there already exist versions of the same technology so advanced, they're practically indistinguishable from magic."

A reference to Arthur C. Clarke, who wrote that any sufficiently advanced technology is indistinguishable from magic.

SCENE 3

"I was on a mission in Belgium once, where the moat was filled with sharks which had Gatling guns grafted onto their heads."

An Austin Powers reference, playing off the bit about "sharks with laser beams attached to their heads."

"Philippe? Philippe Pétain?" said Curie.

Philippe Pétain would have been thirty-three years old in 1889, but during World War II he was the Chief of State of Vichy France, a German collaborator. He was tried and convicted for treason after the war, which informs his "I was just following orders" comment.

SCENE 5

A thick lit cigar dangled from the corner of his mouth.

Nothing to see here. Sometimes a cigar is just a cigar.

"When Al grows up, we shall rule Europe as father and son!"

One more *Star Wars* reference, for good measure.

"Super-smart teenage military commanders? There's something to this…"

And a nod to Orson Scott Card's *Ender's Game*.

SCENE 6

"I'm not that kind of doctor."

Not a reference to any one specific book or movie, but a nod to a very common trope across genres and stories, where a character with some sort of PhD is asked for medical help. (Examples I can think of include *Stargate SG-1* and *Treasure Planet*.)

"Mmmm, pie…" said Al."

A variation of Homer's favorite line from *The Simpsons*.

The young Albert Einstein waved back.

There's a widespread belief that Einstein was a bad student, almost developmentally delayed, when he was young. This is, in fact, not true at all. He was a very bright child and got good grades, though he may have had some disciplinary problems early on, which are common among smart children who get bored easily in class.

Even so, playing off this historical fallacy worked perfectly for my plot. This way I can claim Freud's mad-scientist scheme had succeeded (though not instantaneously, as he had hoped) in producing one of the greatest geniuses of the 20th century.

$E = mc^2$

EXPLAINING CTHULHU TO GRANDMA

A sample from Alex Shvartsman's award-winning short story

I JUST MADE THE DEAL OF THE YEAR and I couldn't wait to tell Grandma.

As soon as the customer left, I locked the front door, flipped the cardboard sign to Closed, and headed into the back. Clutching my latest acquisition to my blouse, I entered the packed stockroom, dodged around the bronze naval cannon, nearly caught the hem of my skirt on a rusty suit of armor, and made my way through a plethora of other items too large or too heavy to be stored on the shelves. Most of this stuff has been here since before I was born, and will likely remain in the same place long after my hypothetical future children take over the shop. You never know when the right buyer might come along, and the family is in it for the long haul.

Grandma Heide was in our office, sitting at the desk. She had moved the keyboard out of the way to make room for the game of solitaire she was playing with a Thirteenth century Egyptian Tarot deck. She barely glanced up when I walked in.

"You do know you could play this *on* the computer, right Grandma?"

She set down a card in one of the columns after a few seconds' thought. "Can your newfangled gadget fake the feel of shuffling a dog-eared deck of cards? Simulate the pleasure of placing one in just the right spot to make a perfect play? I didn't think so." She looked at me over her glasses. "The old ways are almost always best."

"Yes, well, I'm not here to argue about that again. Guess what I just picked up on pawn."

I stepped closer and placed a pocket dimension in front of Grandma. It looked like a pyramid-shaped snow globe the height of a soda can. It was filled with ocean water. In the center floated a being of scales and tentacles and shapes so unnatural that staring straight at it caused a headache. When not stored outside of our space/time continuum, it was the size of a cruise liner and must have weighed as much as a small mountain, which is what made pocket dimensions so darn handy.

Grandma picked up the pyramid, pushed the glasses up her nose and peered inside.

"What is this?" she asked.

"Cthulhu," I said, smug with satisfaction.

"*Geshundheit*," said Grandma. I couldn't tell for certain if she was kidding or not. Probably not.

"I didn't sneeze," I said. "Its name is Cthulhu. It is an ancient god of anxiety and horror, dead but dreaming."

Grandma didn't appear impressed. "What does it do? Besides dream." She turned the pocket dimension slowly to examine its contents.

"Do? It's a symbol for the unknowable fathoms of the universe which dwarf humanity's importance. Besides, it's a god. How long has it been since we had one of *those* in the shop?"

"1982," she said immediately. "The government of Argentina pawned a few of the Guarani nature gods to help fund the Falklands conflict. Little good it did them."

I didn't remember this, but I was still in diapers in 1982.

"Pre-Columbian godlings barely count. This," I pointed at the pyramid, "is the real deal."

Grandma finished inspecting the god and placed the pocket dimension on top of the computer, next to a mug filled with ballpoint pens. She turned her attention back to me.

"And what did you pay out for this rare and unique item?"
I told her.

Grandma pursed her lips and stared me down. Ever since I broke the wing off the stuffed phoenix when I was a little girl, it had been the withering expression Grandma Heide reserved for when I screwed up especially badly.

"Whoever pawned it will have taken the money and run," she declared. "They won't be back. Enjoy it for the next month, and let's hope some fool gets as excited about this overgrown octopus as you did. If not, then maybe we can sell it off by the pound to the sushi chains."

"You never have any faith in the deals I make." I crossed

my arms. "I'm not a little girl anymore, and I spent my entire life around the shop. When will you begin to trust my judgment? I say we got a bargain and I'll prove it."

"This shop is full of the mistakes of overeager youth, Sylvia." She pointed toward the stock room, brimming with stuff. "I made my fair share when I was your age. The pawn shop business is simple. Stick to quality common items that are easy to move, and pick them up cheap. The sooner you accept that, the sooner you'll be ready to take over the family enterprise." Then she drew the next card from her deck, indicating that the conversation was over.

When your family is in the business of running the oldest pawn shop in the world, there are big shoes to fill. I wondered if Grandma had similar trouble when she became old enough to work at the shop, back before Gran-Gran Hannelore had retired.

Under the terms of the pawn, the customer had thirty days to come back and claim his item. That gave me plenty of time to line up potential buyers. There were a number of leads for me to pursue, but I started with the obvious.

I unlocked the front door, flipped the sign to Open, powered up my laptop, and logged on to Craigslist.

Continue reading this and 39 other short stories in

EXPLAINING CTHULHU TO GRANDMA AND OTHER STORIES
UFO PUBLISHING, FEBRUARY 2015

Available in trade paperback, e-book and audio book formats.

"Wit, sentiment, imagination—Alex Shvartsman's got them all." -*Mike Resnick, Hugo award winner.*

"Fantastic variety and scope ... Prepare to be entertained, delighted and amazed." -*Esther Friesner, Nebula award winner.*

"His stories feature tightly constructed, intricate, puzzle-like plots with clever banter and plenty of fresh, twisted pop culture references." -*Ken Liu, Hugo and Nebula award winner.*

"Full of intriguing ideas and wit." -*Jody Lynn Nye, bestselling author.*

"A wonderful collection of short stories that will make you laugh, think and feel." -*Gini Koch, bestselling author.*

ABOUT THE AUTHOR

Alex Shvartsman is a writer, translator, anthologist, and game designer from Brooklyn, NY. Over 80 of his short stories have appeared in *Nature, InterGalactic Medicine Show, Galaxy's Edge, Daily Science Fiction,* and many other magazines and anthologies. He is the winner of the 2014 WSFA Small Press Award for Short Fiction.

Alex edits the Unidentified Funny Objects annual anthology series of humorous SF/F.

His collection, *Explaining Cthulhu to Grandma and Other Stories,* was published in February 2015. His website is www.alexshvartsman.com

Made in the USA
Monee, IL
13 May 2025

17385127R00066